Advance praise for *Qualities of Light*

"*Qualities of Light* is a coming-of-age story replete with lyrical and marvelous detail. Mary Carroll Moore succeeds brilliantly at showing how easily the fragile bonds of family can be torn apart—and how they can be restored by honesty and forgiveness. In one momentous summer, Molly Fisher discovers that the world is not black and white, and her struggle makes her a heroine any reader will remember long after the last page is read."

—Lori L. Lake, author of many novels including the 2007 Golden Crown Literary Society "Goldie" Winner *Snow Moon Rising*

"Mary Carroll Moore's skill as a painter blends beautifully with her sensitive portrayal of first love in *Qualities of Light*. She successfully layers Molly Fisher's many struggles—guilt surrounding her brother's accident, frustration that she and her father don't understand each other, and confusion over where she fits in a group of lake friends. Shining through these layers are Molly's vivid voice and her deepening love for a young woman named Zoe. Moore's skillfully crafted novel both moves and entertains as she follows Molly's summer journey."

—Catherine Friend, author of *Hit by a Farm*, *The Crown of Valencia*, and other books

"*Qualities of Light*, by Mary Carroll Moore, isn't just a beautifully nuanced contemporary lesbian romance, but a sensitive exploration of the cruelty and kindness—the intricate balancing act—that is family love. I couldn't recommend it more highly."

—Ellen Hart, author of twenty-one mystery novels, five-time winner of the Lambda Literary Award, two-time Minnesota Book Award winner for Best Crime and Detective Fiction; author of the Jane Lawless Mystery series.

Qualities of Light

Mary Carroll Moore

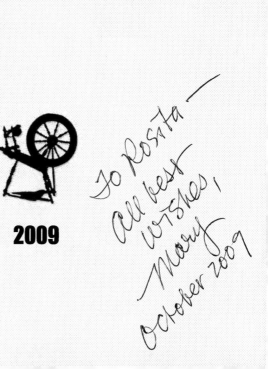

2009

To Rosita —
All best
wishes,
Mary
October 2009

Author's Note: Although some of the Adirondack towns and communities in this story are loosely based on real places I have lived in and loved, I changed significant details to make them fictional. Any resemblance to real locations or to real persons, living or dead, is purely coincidental.

There's a real Daggett Lake water skiing competition each summer. I attended it once in the rain, but it's completely fictionalized for this novel.

Copyright© 2009 by Mary Carroll Moore

Spinsters Ink
P.O. Box 242
Midway, FL 32343

Printed in the United States of America on acid-free paper

First Edition Spinsters Ink 2009

Editor: Katherine V. Forrest
Cover designer: Stephanie Solomon-Lopez
Cover photo credit by eacheric

ISBN-10: 1-935226-06-1
ISBN-13: 978-1-935226-06-2

About the Author

Mary Carroll Moore teaches creative writing at the Loft Literary Center in Minneapolis, the Hudson Valley Writers' Center near New York City, and The Studios at Key West. Her eleven published books include *How to Master Change in Your Life: Sixty-seven Ways to Handle Life's Toughest Moments* (Eckankar Books), *Cholesterol Cures* (Rodale Press), and the award-winning *Healthy Cooking* (Ortho Publications). *Your Book Starts Here: Create, Craft, and Sell Your First Novel, Memoir, or Nonfiction Book*, based on her How to Plan, Write, and Develop a Book™ writing workshops, will be released in 2010. A former nationally syndicated columnist for the *Los Angeles Times*, Mary's essays, short stories, articles, and poetry have appeared in literary journals, magazines, and newspapers around the U.S. and have won awards with the McKnight Awards for Creative Prose, *Glimmer Train Press*, the Loft Mentor Series, and other writing competitions. She lives with her family in Connecticut and New Hampshire and writes a weekly blog for book writers at http://howtoplanwriteanddevelopabook.blogspot.com.

Acknowledgments

A big thank you to skilled editor Katherine V. Forrest and visionary publisher Linda Hill for believing in this story.

Much gratitude to the supportive community of writers, instructors and students at the Loft Literary Center and the Hudson Valley Writers' Center. Thank you to the wise teachers who added to my writing toolbox over the years, especially my advisers in the M.F.A. program at Goddard College—Jan Clausen and Rebecca Brown—where this novel began. I treasure the creative and extraordinary women who came to the Eagle that pivotal August week to share their hearts by the fire and listen to the first story about Molly and Zoe. Thanks also to extraordinary writing instructor Alison McGhee, whose excellent "object" exercise led to the idea of Sammy's jackknife. Appreciation to Minneapolis' own Thursday Night Writers, who sat patiently through many early drafts of these chapters; the Saturday writers from Dunn Bros. Coffee in Minneapolis, an unfailingly supportive group (especially Ellen Grady and Mary Sue Lobenstein, who read final drafts); writers Barbara Buckner, Nancy McMillan and Linnie York, who delivered enthusiastic feedback under deadline; and friends and family who kept me going to the finish line.

I couldn't have done this without Joan and Harold, who taught me why good editing leads to good writing. Or my beloved families, past and present, who believed in me. Or Becca, who always holds my heart and vision in her loving hands.

For my new family, with love

Approach your subject in all humility and reverence—make yourself highly sensitive to its beauty.

Charles W. Hawthorne
Hawthorne on Painting

There are moments in our lives, there are moments in a day, when we seem to see beyond the usual. Such are the moments of our greatest happiness. Such are the moments of our greatest wisdom. If one could but recall his vision by some sign. It was in this hope that the arts were invented. Sign-posts on the way to what may be.

Robert Henri
The Art Spirit

Prologue

Weeks before my little brother Sammy got lost, his voice took on the clarity of a boy soprano. He was six that summer, and he liked to lie in the dirt under our Adirondack cabin, singing. Sound rang through the wide plank floors, eerie and angelic, stirring the heated air.

I lay on my bed in the hot afternoon, reading the same sentence of *Anna Karenina* five times before I went downstairs to quiet Sammy, knowing he'd start again as soon as I went away. He sang at night too, a high hum from his bed across the room. I fell asleep to my brother's music and the clink of my mother making ice in the kitchen.

Down the hill from our cabin, Cloud Lake made its own music. It lapped the rocks and shimmered—dark at night, blue and sharp in the still heat of day. It waited for clouds to pass, to reflect themselves in its flat surface. Although I didn't know it then, that summer I too waited for any impression, my heart as expectant as unmoving water.

Three months from sixteen, I was only beginning to sense

where I was located inside my life. But I always knew where Sammy was.

I couldn't imagine not hearing him.

Chapter 1

My brother lay surrounded by white, the steel-railed hospital bed too big for his small body. The edge of his ear, his cheek, were flushed, like a little kid got after dreaming. My inhale from the doorway hurt my throat. I waited for him to turn toward me and sit up. But Sammy was quiet, one foot exposed, one shoulder, thin and bony in Superman pajamas, barely lifting the sheet.

My mother sat slumped to half her height in a plastic chair. Her feet were the only thing moving, little jerks like she wanted to run. When she saw me in the doorway, a tremor ran through her, shaking the chair to a sudden squeak. She stood up to hug me, her face wet. My dad didn't move. He was by the window, studying the black parking lot, still wearing the sweats he'd slept in.

Aunt Anna nudged me. I walked over, my weighted feet a few seconds behind my body. Sam's chest went up and down, the monitors beeped, his long eyelashes flickered on his cheeks. From outside the window came the muffled traffic of Plattsburgh, the shriek and fade of an ambulance siren. Someone ran fast down the hall. I moved to cover Sam's toes with the blanket.

"Sam's heart is beating normally," the ICU doctor had told us last night, after ten hours. "His vital signs are excellent. We got him off oxygen. But we expected him to wake up by now."

My mother's voice had been irritated. "He's sleeping. What's wrong with that?" She sat up taller, shrugged off my father's hand, her long braid of white-blond hair stark and fluorescent down her back.

"We're wondering if he hit his head on something," said the doctor. He towered above us, stifling a yawn. "Maybe the side of the boat?" My dad's eyes slid toward me.

"My brother. . ." I began.

"Is just sleeping," my mother interrupted. "Sleeping is normal for a six-year-old. Seven, today." Gentle fingers touched my arm as she turned to smile at me, celebrating Sam's birthday.

I closed my eyes. I wanted to shake my brother, tell him to stop fooling around.

In another life, Sam and I were still on Cloud Lake. Before I tried to show off, before the moment when I swerved the motorboat, cut through the sparkling waves.

The doctor went out to a vending machine in the hall. The machine sloshed, and the smell of coffee filled the air. When he came back in, sipping, his erect posture had fallen into an apologetic slump.

After my Aunt Anna brought me home from the hospital Tuesday morning, I stood alone on the cabin's wraparound porch, listening to crows call warnings from the pines overhead, studying my still life.

It was a small painting, of a single pear lying on its side against an old lilac sweater of my mother's, tilted as if it would tumble. I had started it Sunday, the day before everything happened. The unsteadiness of the pear, the suppressed movement, the colors glowing in the morning light had drawn me, but now it was as jumbled as my mind.

Still lifes are a painter's scales. My dad had taught me this early, his big hand guiding my small one as soon as I was able to firmly grasp a stick of pastel. His delight in my early attempts and his belief in me buoyed my life, and without complaint I'd painted a solitary apple twelve times until I saw enough nuances of line and form to please him. I thought it right that only then was I allowed a landscape.

It was worth learning still life first, my father said. Painters faked landscapes all the time, but skill was immediately seen in a still life.

The crows crowded the feeder hung from the eaves of the porch and I waved them away. They rose cawing into the cedar-scented heat of the June morning, circling toward the lakeshore where the water pounded rough against the rocks.

I pushed my glasses up on my nose, trying to see better. That was something else I'd lost yesterday. They lay somewhere at the bottom of Cloud Lake, covered in silt. This spare pair was way too small, perched like an old lady's spectacles. I adjusted the earpieces for a few minutes, then I took them off.

Blurry was easier.

I'd just finished a second piece of toast and another fifteen minutes of discouraged staring at my still life, when I heard footsteps on the cabin path.

My aunt had brought my cousin, who carried groceries from Price Chopper in Plattsburgh. Sarah dumped two bags, settled in the most comfortable chair, and pulled nail polish and *Jane* out of her bag like she lived here. I said hi and went to help Anna with groceries. Anna didn't say anything but gave me a hard hug, took one bag to the kitchen.

"Hey, I'm sorry about Sammy," Sarah said. She did look sorry, for a few seconds. "Hey," she said again, "you remember Chad Anderson?"

Anna and I looked quickly at each other; I looked away first.

"Yup," I said. "I remember Chad."

"He's back on the lake and he's playing at the Boat House Friday night," Sarah said. "I'm doing sound. You should come."

"I may be needed here."

"Why?"

"Sarah!" Anna shook her head.

"I don't know," I said.

"I'll pick you up," Sarah said, like she was doing me a favor.

"You don't drive."

Sarah grinned. "I do, actually. I got my license yesterday. While you were at the hospital. Get this, I almost drove over this cop's foot!" She lifted one tiny black sandal. "They wanted me to wear real shoes. I told them these were from Milan, and it was in Italy, so that made them real shoes."

"Heaven help us," my aunt said, but she wasn't smiling.

"So you should come Friday," Sarah said. "I need practice with real passengers."

I sank into a chair and put my feet on the table, staring at my father's blue coffee mug, unwashed from the day before. It communicated a shivery image of driving with Sarah and talking to Chad Anderson, who knew about everything that had happened.

"You could dance," Sarah said. "I bet Chad would ask you."

No, he wouldn't. I rocked my chair on its back legs, the motion soothing the even worse image of the crowded room of the Boat House—having to smile for hours at one of the booths, sitting alone at the bar, trying to make a Coke last all evening.

"Friday may not work," I told Sarah. "I've got stuff to do."

My bare foot was trying to dance on the table's edge, balance my chair, and find warmth in a moving patch of sunlight. Almost without thinking, I let it contact my dad's favorite mug, feeling the glazed surface.

My cousin tapped long nails on the counter. "You always make life so complicated, Molly Fisher. A person could drive to Albany and back in the time it takes you to make a simple decision."

I nudged the cup to the floor. Blue chips flew. We all looked down at coffee pooling on weathered wood. My aunt bent with paper towels, her eyes understanding.

"Go, Molly," she said. "It'll do you good to get out."

"It'll be fun," Sarah said.

The broken cup made me feel better. Friday was three days

away. Sam would be awake by then. And I didn't have to dance. "Okay," I said. I could sit. Just for an hour.

Sarah stood up, thumping her magazine against her leg. "I'll pick you up at seven. Bring twenty bucks."

"Maybe I should stay home," I said, suddenly afraid. "Dad might need me."

Anna was bundling a wad of brown-stained paper towels toward the trash. She glanced up at me and slowly shook her head. Of course my father didn't want me around.

That afternoon, I crept under the cabin. Behind the woodpile I found the flattened dirt where my brother liked to hide, the small metal box I had given him for his birthday treasures. The latch was rusted and dirty, but I pried it open with a thumbnail.

The box was empty.

I had imagined finding something precious, something I could return to its rightful place. The cache by the lakeside boulder was empty too. I realized my brother had moved on to new hiding places.

I would have to search harder.

Chapter 2

The Friday night band was just warming up. Sarah walked over to the Boat House's sound board, a dinky thing on a folding table, and waved to Chad Anderson. I found a stool at the bar and ordered a Coke, amusing myself by pinching the end of my straw hard and willing it to break enough to allow the tip of my fingernail into the gap. Across the room Sarah was telling a story, high and fast, and I heard Chad's answering laugh.

Chad was taller than me, with a high forehead and thin callused fingers from years of guitar playing. He was wearing neat jeans, deck shoes and a faded blue T-shirt. He hadn't looked over yet. I was glad. I always felt gawky around Chad, as if I were operating with a deliberately simple vocabulary. And I certainly didn't want to discuss the accident.

I leaned over the bar, watching Lester, the Boat House's owner, fill the Coke machine with a huge plastic bag of syrup. The bar was laminated and cool. I laid my cheek on its smooth surface, resting, but my glasses bit against my nose so I slid them off. Even without them, I could read the pennants and bumper stickers and sailing awards Lester had embedded into the bar top. "Cloud Lake Regatta, 1968, J-class." "I Climbed Whiteface Mountain." I traced the letters with a wet finger. The band played a warm-up song, stopped in mid-phrase, someone called to Chad at the sound board that the backup singer hadn't arrived yet. It was a soothing cacophony and I closed my eyes and began drifting off.

"Molly."

Chad was blurred but I recognized the deep voice. Understood the hesitance.

I sighed, put my glasses on. "Chad." I gave him a little smile as if we had no history. "Good to see you."

"How's Sam?"

"The same."

"How are you doing?" The hesitation again. "I got my sweater back."

I gestured toward the stage. "Aren't you playing tonight?"

"After they warm up."

The bass player went wild in a brief solo as the song finished. Kids from the booths clapped, and someone sent a wolf whistle toward Lisa, the lead singer.

Chad leaned closer. "I've been dreaming about it. Really weird underwater dreams." He twirled the straw in his glass. Brown bubbles fizzed their way to the top. "I'm trying to swim up, I can see the sky kind of shining up there above the top of the water, but I can't get my leg free from those rocks."

Each of his words was like a rock, my brain was translating so slowly. I couldn't make sense of any of it, just felt that now-familiar memory, the sensation of a motorboat turning slowly, spinning faster and faster.

"Sing along if you know this one," Lisa purred into the mike.

I turned to watch Sarah at the sound table, talking with a girl I didn't recognize. Like Sarah, she had bright red hair but this new girl was taller and thinner, more athletic, wearing a short dress, clingy like nylon.

"And then last night . . ." Chad said.

"Who's that?" I interrupted, pointing.

"Where?"

"Talking to Sarah."

Chad stared at the new girl. "Haven't seen her around here. I'd probably remember."

The drummer began a solo. Lisa jumped off the stage and ran over to the sound table. Chad and I watched the three of them point to the sliders, laugh. Lisa grabbed Sarah's new friend and pulled her on to the dance floor.

The red-haired girl danced like nobody I'd ever seen. She went by me in a blur of color, completely uncontained, the dress riding up her legs when she turned. Chad and I both stretched our necks, craning to see more. Her mouth was open, laughing; her arms were olive-colored with tan, the red hair like the bright field spots of Indian Paintbrush flowers we get in August, shaking all over her shoulders, long enough to tie back, loose as the wind.

Lisa moved closer, gyrating a little with her hips like she was trying to pull the red-haired girl toward her. They didn't touch; the drummer was hammering way too fast for that.

The red of the girl's lips against the red of her hair almost clashed, like when you see a woman with dyed hair and orange lipstick pushing a pink stroller through Kmart, and the color combination almost blinds you. Her lips were slightly parted, waiting; she was breathing fast from the music and the hot dancing.

She could dance, that girl.

I hadn't danced since last winter, when my dad, on a bad painting day, told me I should lose some weight. But the urge to move was almost unbearable. The arches of my feet ached and my thighs shifted, the blood in them pumping hard. I slid to the edge of the stool, toes almost touching the wide scuffed boards of the floor.

Suddenly, the drum solo ended. Lisa leapt back onstage. The red-haired girl stood, panting, then as if she could tell we were watching, turned and smiled in our direction. She was pretty tall, not as tall as my mother, but taller than me by about half a head. I looked down at my Coke.

Until I felt heat near my shoulder. Movement of air that made me grip myself into stillness.

"Hey," a voice said. A new voice, deep and rich. "I'm not from around here, trying to find this town...Wilmington."

I looked up finally, although I knew it would be her.

"Wilmington's pretty close." Chad's voice was loud in the sudden silence from the stage. He flushed. "Not far from here at all. I know how to get there."

Lester set an iced tea in front of the girl. "Nice dancing."

She nodded, picking up the glass. Her hands were thin with long blunt fingers, a white web between the fingers where the tan didn't reach. "Can I have some lemon?" she asked, smiling at Lester. He looked dazzled, went toward the kitchen.

"Lester doesn't do lemons," I told her, "just so you know."

The girl leaned closer. I breathed in her sweat and the smell of the lake, a scent that hung on all our skins, its weedy sweetness unmistakable and pleasant like the faint memory of sun gone behind clouds. Her skin smelled even more like the lake than mine, as if steeped as tea.

"I noticed you watching us."

Startled, I looked up. Her face was only inches from mine.

"Do you dance?" She was smiling and serious all at once, as if she'd asked, "Do you believe in world peace?" This close, I could see her eyes were gray, a color as unusual as my own, a color that calmed the clash of red hair and lips enough to make harmony in her face. I flushed, looked around wildly, wondering what to say. *Yes, I dance, I love dancing. No, I can't, not until my brother wakes up.* The band's warm-up tune got louder, noise making it hard to think. Dozens of feet began pounding the old wood floor of the Boat House as everyone else started moving to the music.

Lester came over with a little plate. On it were four slices of the yellowest lemon I'd ever seen. He set it in front of the girl.

"I don't know," I almost shouted.

"Wilmington's pretty close to here," Chad said again.

"It's the home of Santa's workshop." My voice cracked, and I cleared my throat, sending this essential information in the direction of the smooth tanned arm.

"Maybe one of you can give me a tour." The girl squeezed two of the slices into her glass, releasing a tang into the air around us, and wiped her hands on her dress.

"I'm sure that can be arranged," said Chad. He smiled at her.

"Hey, Chad," Lisa sang from the stage, "get your ass over here and play."

The girl was leaning even closer to me, studying the decals on the bar by my elbow. "What's a J-class?"

"Sailboat."

"I don't sail. Way too risky." She took a big drink of iced tea. "I waterski. I need someone to drive my boat tomorrow. And a skier to practice crossovers with."

"I've driven boats since I was ten," Chad said.

All this fast talk was making the skin on my face tight. The girl's skin was relaxed, translucent, little veins pulsing near her eyes. Her hair was messed up as if she didn't care about it. As if she didn't have to.

"Do you ski?" she asked, studying me back.

"I used to," I said. "I used to love going out in boats."

"You get *behind* a boat," Chad said gently, "in the water."

"I can get in the water," I said.

"Good." The girl nodded and stuck out one hand. I grabbed it. It was strong and lean, wet from her glass. "I'm Zoe Novato." It sounded Russian.

"Hi," I said. "I'm Molly." My glasses were sliding down my nose. My last name, *Fisher*, seemed way too ordinary.

"Molly Fisher." Zoe looked over at the sound board. "Your cousin told me."

Sarah was waving at Chad, the band's warm-up almost over.

"I'm supposed to be up there," Chad said. "And I can drive your boat for you."

"I'm supposed to be learning the sliders," Zoe said. "And I'll see you both tomorrow. Saturday." We nodded. "The dock at eight? Sarah told me which one's yours."

Sarah had quite the mouth. "Yeah," I said. "Just look for three birch trees leaning in the water."

Chapter 3

I left while the glint of the lake still shone between the trees and lit the shoreline road. The sun was setting, the air quiet, but I walked fast to ease my belly, which felt tenser than it had since the accident five days before. I climbed the steps into the cabin, called hello, but no one answered.

I noticed my father had arranged a parade: eight of Sammy's toys marched across the mantel, frozen in position, waiting for music. I could hear my father outside somewhere, splitting wood. The whimsical mantel parade reminded me I once liked him, how only that winter he'd brought me a thermos of cocoa to stay toasty as we painted hills pink in sunset light.

When I walked down to the lake, I found him. He was standing near the campfire ring, a breeze wafting his hair into little peaks as he worked, his face shadowed by his cap. He chopped so fiercely at the pile of kindling I thought the axe handle would break. I started to turn back then chided myself. I could at least help him. So I came closer, began gathering the pieces and stacking them under the porch.

Late June twilight wrapped around us. We didn't talk, and it was almost companionable, almost peaceful, if I ignored the sound of the axe. It made me jump each time, even though I prepared myself.

"Tomorrow's June twenty-first," I said, just to make conversation. "The longest day of the year. We could have a campfire." It sounded stupid, even to me.

My father grunted. *Thwack* went the axe.

"Dad," I tried again, standing a ways back. "I wanted to talk to you about my painting."

"What about it?"

I searched quickly. "The new still life. It's hard. I wanted to ask you some questions about the cast shadows."

A log split neatly and pieces tumbled onto the dirt. In the near dark, I felt for them. "Remember how you told me the shadows have layers? I guess I'm confused about how to see the second layer." He wasn't looking at me, not even pretending to be interested. So I tried another tack. "I may need you to show me again. Tomorrow?"

"Life is not something anyone can plan right now." Wood splintered. "With the hospital schedule."

I knew this, but someone else had taken over my mouth. I wanted so much, but I couldn't even say what it was exactly. "The blue of this cloth is just like the lake," I babbled on, my breath getting shallower with each word. "I thought you could teach me how to paint the layers of blue, maybe down at the dock. We could even take the boat out." I stopped, finally aware that my father's body was still, the axe frozen on the chopping block, waiting.

"Everyone needs to stay clear of that boat. It's off limits." In the dimness I could see my father's mouth barely moving, a tight line, like the axe had split his face in half too, and soon the two pieces would separate.

"I know. I will." My head bent. Tears began dripping onto my crossed arms. "Daddy?"

"What?" He bit the word, not looking at me.

"I'm really, really sorry."

My father sighed, silent for a minute. Both of us stared at the darkening circle of dirt where white oblongs of freshly split birch lay scattered like broken limbs. "I know you are," he said finally. But he shook his head as he said it, and I knew that being really sorry wasn't nearly enough. He grasped the axe, more gently this time, and set a new birch log on the stump.

The axe cracked into the wood and splinters flew.

Chapter 4

The night before the accident, one of those warm June evenings that promises summer in a north country longing for it, my brother and I had met after dinner at the big granite boulder that jutted into the lake. It was half hidden by the three fallen birches. The trees were still attached to the shoreline, still living, even though their branches dragged the water. My father threatened to cut them down each summer, but I loved their graceful droop.

When I arrived, Sammy was already there, the jackknife in his hands. I sat down next to him, lichen scratchy under my thighs.

"Mom and Dad know," I said. "You've got to stop this." I looked out at the lake, trying to think how to explain it to him. He was so smart in so many ways, but innocent as a baby in others. "Stealing's not Okay, Sammy."

Sunset light reflected off the darkening lake and glinted on his bent blond head. "I'm not stealing," he said. "I always give things back."

I thought of his cache of shiny coins, the old whistle, a spoon my mother never missed. My father's jackknife.

"The other stuff was small. That knife will get us both in trouble."

Sammy shook his head, back and forth, a stubborn drumbeat. "Dad promised. He's giving it to me for my birthday tomorrow."

I knew about this. "You just don't get it," my mother had been whispering to my father that afternoon from the sleeping porch next to mine. Everything was normal then, no hospital schedule to keep us missing each other.

"I think I know what's safe for my own son." My father's voice.

"How would you? Your attention is everywhere but on this family." I could hear the tears in my mother's throat. "How about something normal? He wants a bicycle."

My father's voice had tracked evenly, enunciating each word like my mother was stupid. "He wants Willie's jackknife. I'd like him to have it. It's not a gun, Kate."

In Sammy's hands the knife turned and shone. The cooling lake gave off a weedy smell of day settling into evening. Across the water, Dougall Mountain was a dark hump against the sky. I watched a heron flap slowly toward the deserted beach at the far end, where driftwood gathered during storms.

"Will Daddy miss it, if I keep it till tomorrow?"

"I don't know," I said. I was tired of the knife, tired of navigating around my moody father. I stood up, brushing my hands on my shorts. "What do you want me to give you for your birthday?"

"A boat ride early in the morning, before everyone is awake." Sammy looked up at me. "Just a little one. Across the lake and back?"

We bounced on the morning waves until my glasses were spattered with spray. Sammy was laughing in the back while I drove, watching the sun come up over the mountains. The light touched the water like shooting stars.

I told myself no one would know. We would have the boat back before breakfast.

I cut the engine when we got close to the far shore. Fishermen were settled in the shallows. The sun hadn't quite reached over here. Rocks and trees were wrapped in mist. A loon yodeled once, and its mate echoed from down the lake.

"Hey, do you think I can spear a fish?" Sammy leaned over and aimed the jackknife at a wave, then rocked his body back into the boat.

"Not likely," I said. He looked little against the stern. His vocabulary was so big but he was still small. "Just stay inside the boat, Okay?"

Dad had cleaned, and I couldn't see the orange life preservers that were usually stuffed under the seats. The wind whipped hair across my face, and Sammy shivered. I moved down to the stern, put a hand on his back and rubbed.

"Happy birthday, kiddo. Are you cold?" I looked down at his feet in pink flip-flops. "Did Mom make you get those?"

He shook his head. "I picked them out myself. And I think I see a fish down there." He leaned out again, plunged the knife toward the water. "Pow!'"

"Whoa, little guy," I said, one hand on the waistband of his jeans. "I'll catch you one from the dock and fry it up for your breakfast. Let's get this baby back before Dad wakes up."

"Meemee?"

"Huh?" I was busy making my way back to the steering wheel. The sun was really coming up now, glinting fierce off everything it touched.

"This is the very best birthday present. Riding with you in the boat."

I turned on the ignition and smiled back at him. "It'll be our secret, Okay? Dad would kill me."

"Okay."

"And you'd better put that jackknife away. He'd kill you too if you dropped it in the water."

It was an easy boat, a Chris Craft we'd owned forever. It smelled of comforting times—suntan lotion and fish and fumes and the lake smell I couldn't ever describe when away from the Adirondacks.

Across the water I saw the three birch trees bowing toward the dock, like long white fingers beckoning us home. *Do something fun for him*, my mind said. So after I pulled out of the shallows and away from the fishermen, I started turning the boat in big circles like a waterskier would fly on.

"Cool," said Sammy, "look!"

A line of red-headed Merganser ducks were bobbing near the middle of the lake. "Hello, ducks!" he called. I turned to smile at him; he was leaning over the side staring at the water.

"I just saw a really big fish. Pow!" he said over the noise of the motor, and lifted his arm.

The sharp sun glinted off an object near the stern. Sammy said something like, "It's gone!" and I thought he was talking about the fish.

Then everything happened at once.

A Jet Ski came out of nowhere, Chad Anderson from next door, showing off. He waved, and I swerved to avoid him. I turned the motorboat back toward familiar shoreline, the three birch trees, the dock about half a mile away now. The rising sun was hitting me full in the eyes. I tried to maneuver past the ducks and the Jet Ski.

Over my shoulder, I called, "Sammy Sam, don't tell Dad I did this."

But I heard only the wind and the Jet Ski. Then I turned back. And my mind began saying *no* over and over.

Chapter 5

Late Friday night, I couldn't sleep. Maybe it was moonlight too bright from the lake, or realizing five days had passed since Sam's accident and he hadn't woken up. Maybe it was my rash promise at the Boat House, to water ski with Zoe Novato the next morning.

I decided to get up and clean.

Our cabin, built in 1927, was typical Adirondack construction—a great room with a stone fireplace flanked by four sleeping porches and a tiny bathroom and kitchen. It always smelled good to me, a honey-sweet odor of aged cedar from the planks that made up its walls. My father had built thin shelves between the open studs and his still lifes and paintings from winter were lined there, snow filling our room even in the heat. I gathered Sammy's books from the rug in front of the fireplace and set them on the shelves next to a row of paintings. Their spines looked cheery and colorful.

After a string of hot days, the air inside the cabin was oppressive and smelled of back-drafted wood smoke. An occasional rumble of night thunder came from near Whiteface Mountain. I thought how cool it would be, lying under the cabin where Sammy liked to sing. I couldn't hear him now, even in my head.

In my hands was a book from *The Berenstain Bears*. Sammy had read them all. I turned to the last page, staring at the happy furry faces, everyone forgiving Sister Bear for something stupid she'd done. I closed it carefully and put it on the shelf.

Toys were stuck in the crevices of the couch, a fire engine buried between two cushions, and I gathered some of these into a basket in the corner. I made sure the toys were not just jumbled in the basket, arranging them almost as carefully as Sammy would play with them, as carefully as the parade my father had made on the mantel.

On the table by the window was a jigsaw puzzle my mother and Sammy had started five days before. I sat there for a while, feeling the night breeze scented with rain, holding a sky-blue knobby piece in my hand, searching for its home.

It must've been two by then. Outside was still. I was dozing off when I felt someone breathing behind me.

"What have you been doing?"

My father's face was creased with sleep. He gestured at the basket of toys, the clean sofa cushions, as if a neat room was criminal activity.

"Picking up stuff," I said.

Then I noticed how hard he was gripping the back of my chair. I could feel his knuckles pressing on my shoulders. I moved forward slightly, out of his way. His face was working. He wasn't even looking at me, just staring at the puzzle table.

My hand, on its own, placed the blue puzzle piece back in the unfitted pile.

My father's hands lifted from my chair, and he shuffled away from the table, closing the door to his room.

I sat there, unmoving. After a moment, I got up and slowly began pulling Sammy's toys from the basket. My face grew wet, my nose began to run as I tried to arrange the toys back in disarray. When the tears got too blinding, I dug for a tissue to wipe my face. I didn't question myself when I pocketed one tiny fire engine. When my hand went again to the bright blue puzzle piece from the table. When I tucked one of Sammy's miniature bears under my arm.

It was quiet on my sleeping porch. The wind was moving the birches outside the screen, thunder now faint in the distance. I put the toys under my pillow. I didn't wonder what I'd do with them. At the time, taking them made perfect sense. Nobody would notice they were gone.

I went out three more times that night, passing through the cabin's main room and putting something more in disarray. The unfinished puzzle, the small pair of swim goggles, the early reader books, the messy basket of toys watched from their respective corners, and I felt the nagging of these things that missed my brother too.

Chapter 6

Even though I hadn't slept much, I was up early Saturday morning. I got eggs from the fridge, put six in a pan of water, lit the propane stove with the fireplace starter, and went into my room to look over my two bathing suits.

A fat strip of sun was working its way along the floor toward my bed. There wasn't much in the room, just Sammy's cot and my double bed, with its old mattress and chenille spread, a card table and two chairs, my bookshelf and dresser, and a poster from the Bolshoi Ballet. On the floor was a rag rug my aunt braided. It was red, with strips of vibrant orange, and it reminded me of Zoe Novato.

I smoothed the bathing suits on the bed and looked at them. They were both awful, in that way of fashion mistakes, where you thought you were being cool and interesting but you really were embarrassing yourself. I pulled on the one with the little skirt that hid some of my thighs, not risking the boy-short bikini. Then I put a pair of jean shorts on top, stuffing the skirt inside until it was as flat as possible.

Zoe would probably tell me I didn't look anything like a waterskier in that skirt. It was the absolute truth.

There was nothing I could do about it except make the best egg salad possible.

The eggs were racketing in their pan and at least ten minutes had gone by, so I drained them and cooled them under the tap and the shells cracked easily. I stirred in curry powder, watching it turn an awesome yellow. Anna had made bread, and we had a new loaf on the counter, so Zoe and I would have great sandwiches. I made three.

When I got to the dock, she was already there. Chad Anderson nodded to me from behind the wheel, his hands relaxed and competent, his eyes curious. I couldn't look at him until my breath came fully again, because for an instant, his hands had turned to white blurs pulling Sammy from the reeds.

Zoe was wearing a bright blue tank suit and shorts like mine. She said hi then kept working intently, one of the skis on her lap. I could smell the Coppertone on her skin from where I stood. Her red hair caught the sun like it was on fire.

I set my bags down on the dock and wondered what to do next. The lake was not inviting, the boat straining the line Chad had tied to the pier. I curled the toes tight in my flip-flops, thinking about stepping onto the rocking gunwales. It seemed impossible.

"You can get in," Zoe said. "I'll be done in a sec." She didn't look like a dancer this morning. She knelt, her legs splayed, and set her booted ski on the bottom of the boat, pushing against the straps with one hand. When she bent over, the tiny bones of her back looked like a ridge of far-away mountains.

"What's all that?" she asked me.

"Lunch."

"We'll be back way before lunch."

But Chad was already on the dock, hefting one of my bags. The bag was a canvas tote from my father, "Art Smarts" printed on the side. Unstable, it tilted and the orange life preserver fell out.

Chad stuffed it back in, not looking at me.

"Any news?" he said softly.

I shook my head. The fleeting glance toward my face was so kind, I knew I'd start crying soon.

"May be a little rough for skiing today," he said, quickly changing the subject.

"Never too rough for skiing." Zoe looked over at me, her face a question. "Molly promised to ski double so I can practice crossovers."

I didn't actually plan what happened next, but as I stepped toward the boat my flip-flop caught on the edge of the Adirondack chair. I stumbled, hit my knee. Immediately a red spot rose.

"Whoa," Chad said, grabbing my arm to steady me. "You Okay?"

"Stupid," I said, making sure I got up slow, limping a little. "Bad timing."

I could feel the burn of Zoe's eyes, so I looked away from her to the other side of the lake, rubbing my knee and staring at the tiny dots of boats on the far shoreline.

"You sure you're Okay?"

"I'll be fine." I waved one hand, winced a little.

"You're not fine enough to ski." Her voice bobbled as a big wake hit the boat and bounced it against the dock.

"I can ski. I want to." I pushed the words toward the far shore. "Chad, you ski. Molly can drive."

"Molly doesn't drive." I looked up quickly. Chad was back in the boat, fiddling with the steering wheel.

Zoe didn't answer, just carefully bent the ski binding until it snapped satisfactorily. She stood, wiping her hands on her shorts, and lay the fixed ski alongside the other two. "Well, I guess that means no crossovers today."

"I can do it." I took a small step forward. The pain in my knee was real.

But Zoe shook her head. "Do you still want to come out with us?" Her voice was kind too, as if she'd heard what had happened and was realizing what it cost me. "It's just a short ride, but you don't have to."

I can't do it, I thought.

"We could park you on the beach, you know." She pointed

toward the far end of the lake. "We're practicing down there where it's calmer."

"Okay," I heard myself say. My glasses were misting from the heat; I couldn't see her eyes that well.

"Good." She stood up. Chad and I were quiet, listening to the waves thump the dock and boat.

"Why do you have three skis?" I finally asked, just to break the silence.

"One is for slalom," Chad said. "This girl can even ski on plywood."

I didn't for one moment believe him but Zoe flushed, like she was pleased. "It just takes a lot of practice," she said. "Anyone can do anything with enough practice."

It took me five minutes just to get in the motorboat. I forced myself to move one foot, then the other, pretending my knee really hurt. Chad and Zoe reached to help me in. I found a seat on a bench near the stern, held on to the sides of the boat, tried to ignore the pitch. Told myself it'd be Okay.

But it wasn't.

My mother was a pilot. When flying through storms, pilots counted to one hundred to keep from getting scared. I slitted my eyes against the wind and reviewed novels I'd read, their placement on the library shelves. I ignored the slap of waves on metal, Cloud Lake's ring of mountains, the water's chaotic blue. When Chad swerved around another boat's wake, I focused hard on my chipped toenail polish, a color Sarah was tired of. I leaned over the side and gulped spray, flooded suddenly with the feeling of Sammy's soft weight in my lap, his giggle as small hands turned the pages of his book too fast and I held them back.

Even with my eyes almost closed, the wind brought stinging tears.

Zoe Novato, standing tall in the bow, swayed like she was on the floor of the Boat House, moving to wild music, as comfortable with the motion of the waves as if she were one herself. At one point, she called to me, "Are you Okay?"

I opened my eyes, nodded. Held on to the vinyl seat and tried to smile back.

And I made it. Soon we were approaching the far end of the lake and the deserted driftwood beach where storms from the south gathered firewood in a heap, where they would leave me while Zoe skied.

Chad slowed the boat and stood up, his bare feet gripping the rubber flooring as he turned the wheel.

I scoped out a big piece of driftwood log near some pale sand, a calm place to read my book. Zoe would probably forget about me. I imagined her dancing away on the waves, loose-limbed and bright against the wind-churned lake; it made me feel relieved and strangely sad. I could still watch her, even if she wasn't my friend. I could eat all the egg salad sandwiches if I got hungry, if she didn't want one.

I told myself I would be fine.

It was getting hot now that we were out of the wind. I started to get up, but Zoe moved first. She bent over her ski collection, solemn with concentration. My bathing suit elastic was digging into my thighs beneath the jean shorts. I ran two fingers along the edge of the vinyl bench, feeling the duct tape Chad's father had placed there, waiting for permission to move or speak. Up at the bow, Zoe said something low to Chad. He laughed, carefully folding his sunglasses and setting them on the dash. I focused on my driftwood log, willing the knot of nausea lower in my gut. Finally Zoe moved toward me, sat down. I tried to scoot over to give her some room, and my thighs released from the plastic with an embarrassing sucking sound. She pretended not to hear.

"Your knee hurt?" She lightly touched the bruised place, her hand spread wide against my skin.

"Yes," I said. Shook my head. Bent my knee to show her it still worked. Sat there, my heartbeat shallow and confused.

"I heard about your brother. I'm sorry."

"Thanks."

There was a pause.

"You still want to sit on the beach and watch?"

I nodded.

Zoe squeezed my arm, her eyes friendly. "We'll do crossovers another day. We have all summer."

A knot inside eased at her words. "I sure messed up your plans."

"Plans change. Hey, you have great color eyes." She peered closer. "Blue but not quite."

"Violet," I said. "It's a recessive gene."

"Wow. Hey, good thing you wore shorts. That sand looks hot." She smiled. "Do you mind wading in? It's too shallow for the boat."

"No problem." I smiled back at her.

"Alrighty then. Let's get this show on the road." She squeezed my arm again and leapt off the cushion, bending to get her skis on. The sun reflected off the smoothness of her tanned back.

Chapter 7

The beach was boring.

I ate all the sandwiches, watched Zoe rise again and again from the water, closed my eyes against the arc and swerve of the boat and its wave-slapping rhythm. Read my book. Dozed until they woke me.

Zoe grinned at me all the way home. She sat across from me, her face turned toward the wind, her eyes half-shut, her palms flat on her knees. Chad had his sunglasses back on. He drove steadily toward our dock but he kept looking back at me, like he was making sure I was Okay.

I held my stomach, uneasy from egg salad, and pretended to admire the mountains, the way light glinted off the lake. I imagined what I'd say if Zoe asked me to come out in the boat again. Later that afternoon, for instance.

But she never did. She didn't even ask if I'd had a good time. They let me off at the dock, and I gathered all my bags and started up the hill to the cabin, listening to Zoe's laughter and the roar of Chad's motorboat fade.

It was hot and still away from the water. I suddenly felt lonely. Pines towering above my head filtered the midday light into patterns on the dirt path, and the humid air felt smeared against my skin. I thought of taking a swim to cool off. I thought of sitting on the dock, waiting for Zoe to circle back. Then I told myself I'd be better after a nap. The strange new hollow in my chest was probably because of the boat ride, too soon after all that had happened that week.

But I knew it was really because of her.

I made myself think of Sammy in his white hospital bed. Maybe he'd woken up while I was on the lake. At the cabin, the door to my parents' sleeping porch was closed, as if my mother was home. A dirty sandwich bag and her coffee thermos sat on the kitchen table. I rinsed both out, set my mother's book bag near their bedroom door, looked around for something else to clean.

I thought of calling Zoe on the phone. "This is Molly Fisher," I could say. "Thank you for the boat ride. I could try crossovers tomorrow." She might have gone back for lunch, since she hadn't eaten my egg salad. She'd mentioned staying with her father at Lester's rental cabins. I could get the number pretty easily.

Then I heard it. A humming sound both muffled and distinct that caused my breathing to hitch.

Sam?

I listened with every cell. It was more of a wail than a song. It lifted and fell, staccato gulps and low moans, like Indian women at a funeral, walking barefoot on a dusty road, beating their breasts. Not a sound Sam would make. It made me shiver.

I slid up to the door, knocked once.

The noise stopped abruptly.

"Yes?" came a muffled voice. My mother.

"Can I come in?"

"Just a minute." I heard a slow shuffle. When the door opened, she stood there in her bathrobe, her bare toes twisted over each other. Her face was blotchy and red, strands of hair pasted wetly to one cheekbone. Her eyes were wild, as if she'd been startled awake. She looked like hell.

Terror rose in my throat.

"Is Sammy Okay? Did he . . ." I couldn't bring myself to say the word *die*.

"Molly, stop shouting. I can hear you." My tall, beautiful mother was pushing hair out of her mouth. "Where have you been?"

"At the dock with friends." Maybe *friends* was too strong a word. With a red-haired girl I just met, I started to say, my spine tightening at the memory of Zoe's hair in Cloud Lake wind.

"I'm going to nap for a while," I said, turning toward my room.

My mother coughed. "Is it raining?"

Her presence in my life had always been less insistent than my father's, probably because she was often in the sky rather than on the ground. But there were things I could always count on, and one was her pilot's awareness of the weather. Sunshine was leaking across the floorboards at my mother's feet. I pointed down.

"It's not raining," I said slowly. "Are you Okay?"

She moved her long toes into the sun, massaging a balled-up Kleenex in her hand. "I thought. . ." Then, squinting at Anna's lamp on the table, "What's that?"

"Aunt Anna got it for twenty-five cents."

"How hideous," my mother said.

My exhale was relieved, her comment reassuringly normal.

"How about I make us both some tea?" I said.

I gently took her elbow, led her to the couch. She moved without resistance, sank down slowly, her body such a collection of long fragile bones, I imagined I could lift her as easily as one of the sticks in the basket by the fire. I left her there, went to the kitchen, lit the burner and filled the kettle. Peered back to check on her; she hadn't moved. I found two big mugs on the counter, orange and green, decorated with goofy dancing cats. Aunt Anna had told me peppermint was good for sadness. Peppermint tea bags were in a box in the cupboard. The water boiled, I brought the mugs in.

My mother took the one I handed her and cradled it.

I sat, watching her, feeling an urge I'd never had. I wanted to pull her against me, hold her like I held Sammy when he cried. She was never still like she was now. My hand almost lifted, almost reached to touch the white-gold of her hair.

But she leaned away from me, shifting her body on the wicker couch, sipping tea determinedly, leaving a thin wetness on her upper lip. "It's way too hot for tea, isn't it."

"It doesn't matter," I said. Down at the lake, a motorboat revved near our dock. I forced myself to taste the tea.

My mother blew at her mug, not looking at me. "Your father and I had another fight."

"About Sammy?" My mother wanted to call in a specialist from Cornell, my father wanted to wait.

"Probably. I don't remember."

My mother turned around as if seeking the distance to the door. She set the mug on the table, unfolded the sodden ball of Kleenex in her bathrobe pocket, carefully blew her nose, and stuffed the tissues between the couch cushions. Her hands suddenly had nothing to do. I watched them circle for a minute, aimless, then flatten on her knees. The first night, in the ICU waiting room, I'd slept against her shoulder, she against mine. Her hands were the same, restless yet precise, used to steering a plane, used to control in dangerous conditions. It was just the rest of her that was different now, held in.

She stared at her fingers. "I can't remember much. Even when I last did my nails." I nodded, as if we both agreed that was important. Then her mouth twisted, and she dove for the tissues again.

"We have more." I reached for the box I knew was on the end table, knocking a cheap china figurine which crashed to the floor.

I handed her the box. "Sorry."

"Anna and her junk stores." She smiled, watery, blew her nose again. Her eyes were clearer. "It was hideous too."

Watching my mother, I felt for my own tears. My eyes had dried in the lake wind, become dazed from Zoe and the reflections of sun on water. My head ached slightly.

My mother put one hand on my knee, palm cool against my heated skin. "You're all burned," she said. "You need aloe on that."

"It'll be Okay."

"I know." She leaned her head on the sofa's wicker headrest, closed her eyes. "Just this morning, I was thinking about that time you were in the pageant."

For a moment, I couldn't follow. *Dancing*, I thought. I shut my ears.

But my mother's voice pursued me. "Outdoors all day. You got lobster red. Sam always browned but my fiery Molly just burns." Her voice got soft, almost as if she were sleep-talking again. "You were graceful as a bird when you danced."

I thought of Zoe's legs flashing under a red dress. The burn in my throat intensified. "I've given up dancing."

"Why would you do that?" She rolled her head, her eyes pinning me.

"I don't feel it anymore."

She shook her head, rolling back to neutral. "Maybe you'll feel it again."

"Maybe," I said.

There was a long pause where I thought about the maybes in my life. How to begin telling her about them. I pressed my palms together. "Daddy was so mad that day," I started. Seeing the question in her face, I hurried on. "Sammy started badgering me to take him out on the boat. Every moment, he kept at it."

My mother's body had stiffened. I could feel her fierce attention and her reluctance. I gave her a moment, picking up my tea and bending my face toward the heat, letting it mist my glasses, my eyes behind them, willing the tears.

"Sammy goes on and on when he wants something really bad. You can't refuse him. You know?"

"I know," said my mother, very softly. Her thumb ran faster circles along the rim of her mug.

"And I know how to drive the boat." I heard the intake of her breath, the sharp cut off of air. "I do. I took that water safety course last summer."

"You did." Her eyes were wetter, her face serious, not shying away anymore. "But bad things happen in an instant, Molly. Anything can happen in an instant."

"And it was Sammy's birthday," I finished. This sounded like the lamest reason of all, even to me. "It was what he really wanted. A ride. With me. And I decided, what's the harm of that?"

We sat in the silence of my bad decision.

"Thank you for telling me," my mother said at last. Her voice was distracted. I watched her eyes scan the walls, my father's still lifes. The small parade of Sammy's toys on the mantel.

She frowned at the mantel. "We should straighten up in here."

"I tried. Daddy stopped me."

"Don't let him stop you."

I set the Kleenex box back on the table. The dustpan was under the kitchen sink, the small hand broom nearby. I brought them in, bent to pick up the pieces of broken china.

"You took the boat out by yourself." My mother gathered herself and bent toward the toys. "Your father's told you a hundred times not to."

I stared at her back, my face hot. "What about the fact that Sammy took. . ." I didn't want to tell her. The jackknife was still Sammy's and my secret. "I wanted you to know I was careful."

My mother reached for a yellow toy truck, two picture books. She walked a few steps, holding them. I stood up, took them from her, placed them carefully in the toy basket. I picked up the broom and dustpan.

"I know you're careful," her voice followed me. "You'd never do anything intentional to hurt Sammy. But what about the things we don't intend? Anyone can crash no matter how experienced. Life is full of big mistakes, things we don't expect to happen."

My mother had never made a big mistake. She'd never crashed her plane, never broken a promise, never lost someone she loved. The china pieces fell together in the trashcan, brittle sounds that hurt my ears.

"I'm hungry," she said, her voice small and surprised. "Did you have lunch?"

"Not yet."

"We'll have hot dogs and talk more." She smiled as if lunch were the practical solution for everything wrong in our lives.

But she disappeared into the bathroom while I was cooking

the hot dogs. When she came out, her eyes were swollen from weeping, her body eerily slack. I helped her back to bed and threw out the hot dogs.

Before I lay down, trying to sleep in the humidity, I found the bottle of aloe vera and slathered it on my legs. It dried slowly, sticky like cellophane.

Chapter 8

When I didn't hear from Zoe that evening or the next morning, I told myself I was relieved. But really what I felt was surprisingly sharp disappointment that she had forgotten about me so quickly.

To distract myself, I took my breakfast to the clearing where I was still trying to paint the single pear.

My mother left, hugging me goodbye. She seemed better. My father came home, said hello but nothing more. I was doing Okay until he walked by again, going toward his studio, still not looking my way. Suddenly I felt the long day ahead. I would be totally alone, with no friends to see, no Sammy, not even my parents around.

Panicked, I called to his disappearing back.

"Dad?"

My father hesitated. I felt his reluctance like a rash sweeping my skin, but it didn't matter. "I'm having trouble with this painting. Can you help?" I wasn't really having any trouble. I'd solved the cast shadow problem and the layering of colors was clicking along.

It took him a year to turn, come over, pause a safe distance from my easel, and study my rough sketch.

"What's your question?"

I thought fast. "The focal point, where it should be."

"Where do you think it should be?"

"Here." I pointed.

He adjusted his glasses, leaned forward. The back of his neck was so familiar, the teacher part of him so much our old ways of being together, I felt happy for a minute. Above our heads, a jay called and a shaft of sun moved, illuminating the pear to near translucency.

"Maybe I started that area too bright."

"It's Okay to start bright." He even smiled a little. "You always do."

"You never do."

He placed a warm palm on my shoulder. "Keep trying to get it. I'll be back later to check on you."

"I'll keep trying," I said, a grin almost exploding from my face.

I watched him walk slowly up the path toward the road. He painted five hours every day, and although the daily hospital time had messed up everyone's routine, he was back at it, wearing his work clothes: jeans and a gray T-shirt, neat as if they had been ironed.

I was glad to see his hair was sticking up in back.

My father was famous long before I was born. Framed awards and magazine articles lined his studio walls. In the photographs he stood dark-haired and pensive, his intense blue eyes turned unflinchingly toward the camera. Even I knew he was incredibly handsome, and I was beginning to realize how much it got him in trouble.

In novels, artists had casual affairs with their models. I knew my father didn't do anything casually, and I knew he loved my mother. I saw the longing on his face when she wasn't looking. But an awkward dance of passion and rejection had built borders between them, like a crooked fence neither wanted to take down.

Since the last portrait which still hung in the cabin, his best painting of her, she refused his pleas to pose for him. She had been my father's only model for most of their marriage. But she didn't like his new paintings; they disturbed her.

That's when I heard them arguing about the new models who began coming to the studio, students from the college in Plattsburgh who posed for his classes. When he painted them late into the evening, I wondered what else they did. Maybe my mother wondered too. I watched her darken inside, cook constantly, fly extra hours in her small plane, escaping to the sky.

My father's last portrait of my mother hung in the main room of the cabin. Skylights over the fireplace pulled sun into the space, lighting her face for most of the morning.

We were all used to my mother's beauty—the high cheekbones, aquiline nose, tiny ears studded with the garnets she always wore—but this portrait didn't deliver beauty. He had captured her on a gray day, sitting on the dock, charcoal sky and green summer trees framing her pale hair—and he had painted the layers of shadow and light only known by someone very close. And very observant.

After that painting, my mother refused to sit for my father.

After that painting, I wondered what he observed in me.

He came out of his studio around four. I heard him in his room, getting ready to leave for the hospital again. I knew he wanted to go alone, but I had given up hope of Zoe coming by or having the courage to call her. I needed to put to rest this new longing, and the morning's conversation with my father had encouraged me. Besides, I told myself, I'd only been to see Sammy three times.

So I walked to my father's truck while he was getting dressed. I was still in my bathing suit and shorts, my thighs crackled with aloe vera, but I didn't care. I sat in the passenger seat, waiting, staring into the late sunlight slanting off the field.

My father paused when he saw me. But he didn't say anything, just got in too.

We drove off.

Dust rose around the fenders of the pickup; I had to keep my window closed all the way to the main road. Along Route 3, I watched the silent mountains, the Saranac River moving slowly alongside, the occasional startle of blue wilderness lakes.

Finally, we were in the evening heat of Plattsburgh.

I left my father at the hospital entrance. Nearby was a science store. Shelves of games, toys and kits for educational projects, plus the biggest collection of stuffed animals in the North Country. My mother shopped there every Christmas for Sammy's presents.

I was going to get Sam a common stuffed animal like a snake. I ended up with a lion. It was small, about the size of my father's hand, with a strong face. The insides filled with heavy beads let it bend and soften. I imagined it could easily be pressed to Sam's cheek, even in sleep. I put it in my backpack, walked back to the hospital, and pushed the button for the fourth floor.

Chapter 9

My mother was reading by Sammy's bed; she looked up and smiled a tiny welcome at me. Her eyes were rimmed with the dark shadows of tears and no sleep.

I gave the lion to Sammy then settled myself on the floor near her.

Hours passed. At one point my mother stood up and walked toward Sammy's bed. She lifted the lion from under his arm and placed it carefully on the bedside table. She stood there for a minute, stroking the golden fur. My father got up and went to her side. He raised his arm, hesitated, then put it around her shoulders. She didn't try to move away.

They bent together over the little table. I watched the solid wall of their backs and felt alone again—and terrified.

By midnight I was shivering. One of the nurses brought me a blanket. My mother finally slept. My father read a book on art history, light from a small lamp encircling his face. I sat and listened to my brother breathe, a soft whistling snuffle that lulled me a little, made me forget.

Once when my father went out to get coffee, I walked over to the bed and stood for a few minutes with my face as close as possible to Sammy. He smelled dry and dusty like the road from the cabin, green like the reeds that grew in Cloud Lake. I put the lion back in the crook of his right arm, away from the IVs, and pulled the covers up. And I swear he moved.

I held my breath, saw the movement again, just a tiny one, then all was still.

We held our silent vigil, my father cocooned by his reading light, my mother by her dreams, me in my blanket. I dozed a little, jerking awake when my head dropped. Nurses slid in and out every few hours, taking vitals. My father turned pages.

I watched him and I watched my mother and mostly I watched Sammy. A memory came to me, like a midnight dream fragment. We were camping together, our annual end-of-summer trek to Listener Pond. Birds twittered and grew silent as the sun set over the small expanse of water. We toasted marshmallows, and in the sterile hospital room I could almost smell the flaming outsides, the burnt soft sugar.

Each year around the campfire at Listener Pond, my family created ghost stories, embellishing even the wildest tales—Meathook Harry, who scratched at screens; pilots who landed on mountainsides and wandered into wilderness camps. And as I sat in Sammy's room, watching his even sleep, I remembered a story my father had told before the winter began.

As a boy, my father had often camped at Listener with his family, but once he went alone. He had been my age, uncertain and directionless.

In the night he'd wandered to the water's edge and fell asleep there. He'd woken before dawn to the sound of footsteps, heavy and rhythmic.

"A monster?" Sammy had held his breath at this point in the story.

My father opened his eyes wide, awed with the memory. "Rabbits," he said.

A group of snow hares, the jackrabbit of the north, had

circled a boulder close to where he slept. He said he'd never seen anything like it, their leaps in the air, their light landings. His voice dropped to a whisper, and we looked out at the pond, wishing for the glint of starlight on fur. My father said that one after another, the rabbits had danced in the moonlight while he stayed as still as possible.

Finally, his leg cramped and he had to move. The rabbits heard him and fled away into the dark.

In the deepest part of that night at the hospital, when I was dreaming about the jackrabbits, I woke to my mother's cries. My father was awake too, alert and staring at her. We both sat motionless, listening. She stirred and woke a little, opening her eyes.

"What?" she said.

"You were talking in your sleep again," I said.

"Did I say anything good?" She smiled a little, but the smile didn't reach her eyes. "I was dreaming of Sam."

Outside, the hospital intercom blared a call. I was suddenly swamped by the smells of death and sickness and stingy antiseptic all around us.

"It's been a week. Oh, God." A long pause, then, "What if he never wakes up?" My mother's whispered, almost unconscious words brought back the memory of her crying from the screened porch.

He moved, I saw it! I wanted to shout, but my father stilled me with a look. I held my breath, watching him.

"That," he said slowly and distinctly, "would be giving up. Nobody's given up."

The clock clicked forward. The intercom page crackled again, calling someone to save a life.

Chapter 10

At seven the next morning, my father woke me. The blanket was twisted around my legs as if I'd been fighting in my sleep. My book was splayed open on the floor beside me. I was very stiff when I stood up.

My father moved quietly around the room, folding his blanket then mine. His satchel stood open on the chair, ready for the book light and empty coffee mug from his night vigil. "Time to get going," he told me, his face weary, eyes desperate for more generous illumination.

My mother's chair was empty. "Don't we need to wait for Mom?" I asked.

"The doctor told her to go home, get some real sleep," my father said, his mouth a tight line, as if he disagreed with both of them. "He'll call us if Sammy's condition changes."

Sun was just coming through the slatted Venetian blinds. My mouth felt dry and I needed a toothbrush and time to wash my face. But as my father was opening the door to the hall, the doctor was coming in. He walked to Sammy's bed, read the chart and let it drop, gave me a nod and drew my father into a corner where they talked for a few minutes, my father asking something urgently. The doctor put his hand on my father's arm, shaking his head. My father looked even more discouraged. Then he nodded, his head bent.

I wanted to tell my father, "Sam moved in the night," but I knew he hadn't stirred again. It had been a week since the accident, time enough for him to wake up. To this end I had watched him so carefully, almost memorizing the lines of his face, the shape of his arms and small hands, as if I were drawing them. But he'd been quiet as a lake at dawn, still gone from us, the rise of the white sheet covering his chest the only witness to his breathing.

The doctor said goodbye and went out.

"What did he say?"

"Nothing's changed."

"Do they think he's going to . . ." I didn't finish, remembering what my father had said in the night. I certainly wasn't giving up.

"I'm going to use the restroom," I said instead.

"Take your time."

I ran water in the sink and splashed my face, keeping the bathroom door open a crack. My father placed our bags by the door and walked over to Sammy's bed. He stood there for a minute, reading the chart as the doctor had done. Then he picked up Sammy's hand, the one that snaked with IV lines. He didn't move it much, didn't raise it too high, just held it gently in the cup of his big hands like it was an injured bird. I flushed the toilet and opened the door, and my father lowered the hand.

"Ready?" he said.

"Almost."

"I'll put this in the truck." He picked up the bags and walked toward the door, saying again, without turning, "Take your time."

When we were alone, I sat on the edge of Sammy's bed, where there was plenty of room. He was breathing regularly, a peacefulness on his face that made him look very old, as if he were seeing in his sleep all the things he wanted to know. I wondered if his dreams would soon be more real than life out here. Would he lie under some cabin in another place, humming softly, and I would be here, unable to listen? Acid traced my throat in a long sear at the thought. I had to swallow hard before I bent to kiss his cheek.

Was it possible only days ago I had worried only about how to tell my parents about Sammy's small thefts? Now I had stolen something you couldn't put back as easily as a knife in a desk drawer.

"Please wake up," I whispered into his ear. *I'm sorry I showed off for you in the boat. I didn't mean for any of this to happen.* "Please wake up." The plea was immediately absorbed by the sterile air. I couldn't even hear Sammy's breathing, although the sheet rose with each inhale.

My face was wet. I wiped tears from Sammy's exposed arm and tucked the arm under the thin covers. My father had moved the stuffed lion so it was clenched again in Sammy's hand.

Seeing the lion held so tightly made me feel a tiny bit better. Maybe part of Sammy was listening. Maybe he had heard me. He would probably be awake soon. To celebrate, I would get him a bear.

After the chilly hospital room, the summer air felt comforting on my skin. My father was idling near the emergency entrance. I got in and rolled down the window and we bounced over speed bumps, out onto the street.

Plattsburgh was quiet, only a few people going to work this early, the day already warm. I leaned my head against the doorframe, letting the wind bat my cheeks and eyelids as my father accelerated. I imagined we lived in northern Russia near the Gulf of Finland, where in summer it's daylight for twenty-four hours and people sleep with shades drawn tight and play in the park at midnight. I liked to think of all that daylight, everyone awake all the time.

Price Chopper was open, clumps of cars in the parking lot. My father came out with orange juice and a Friehofer's coffee cake. We traveled along Route 3. The sun was bright on the river, and when my dad noticed it, he started whistling, like he was remembering his studio and finally had permission to be cheerful.

Above the rush of wind blowing past our faces, we listened to public radio, a discussion on acid rain, the local weather. It was a good day for hiking, and you could see the White Mountains from the top of Marcy. "How about that," my father said.

But Marcy, the highest peak in the Adirondacks, seemed far away to me. I wondered about closer things.

If Zoe was skiing out on the lake.

If I would let myself eat coffee cake for breakfast.

If my brother would wake up tomorrow, or the next day.

When we got back to the cabin, my father parked the truck near his studio.

"I'm going for a walk," he said, but his fingers stayed on the door handle. The sun glinted so sharply off the hood, I had to squint to see him. "Do you want to come?"

I started to answer, "Sure."

Just then I heard a girl's voice, calling high from a neighboring dock, then the sound of a boat starting. I jerked toward it, my face surely hopeful, and I saw my father's lips press together.

"Maybe later," I said. "I want to sit here a minute."

"Maybe later then." He got out of the truck and closed the door quietly. I watched him go down the hill toward our cabin.

It was silent. Every now and then I could hear wind whooshing the tops of the white pines. The boat sound was gone now. The sun was strong and my eyes hurt. I sat there, staring at my father's studio, and for some reason I got out of the truck, closed the cab door quietly, and walked over.

The key was on its nail. The door opened easily. I stood, inhaling the slightly sweet odor of the soft pastels, lemony like furniture polish, the dusty air. The smell and quiet of the room were familiar, comforting, waiting for my father and his stirring attentions.

On the larger easel, a sheet of paper hung, white and waiting, its corners taped neat and cut on the ends. A half-finished portrait of a black-haired woman was balanced on the windowsill. I started to walk over to look.

Then I noticed the sketches.

Arranged on the table, in pale colors, were five portraits of Sammy. I recognized the hospital bed, the flat curve of its headboard and the side railing they put up so he wouldn't roll to the floor. Sun slanted across the table and caught Sammy's hair and sleeping face in a halo of light.

The sketches were so gentle and accurate they made my throat close up.

After a few minutes, I slid my way out of the room and shut the studio door.

Once when I was five, we arrived home late from an art show opening in Lake Placid. My mother had dressed me in red velvet and new patent leather Mary Janes. The slippery bottoms of my shoes delighted me, and I skidded merrily across the gallery floor until my father scooped me up and snuggled me in his big arms. "My daughter Molly," he told prospective buyers, "the other artist in the family." I buried my face in his neck, breathing the dusty artist scent of him.

I fell asleep in his arms and stayed asleep through the ride home, tucked in the backseat under a comforter my father had thought to bring for me.

When I got out of the car, sleepy and confused, I stumbled into a patch of barbed wire that lay next to the greenhouse. My mother had already gone into the house to turn on lights, and it was my father who held me as I wailed. He warmed milk in a bottle for me that night, even though I was way too old for such care. When I finally fell asleep, my cheeks still glazed wet from tears and warm milk in my belly, I listened to the sound of my father humming under his breath, the familiar scritch of his pencil skittering over a sketch pad as he sat by my bedside all night.

Even as I got older, I wanted to be exactly like my father. I rejoiced at what we shared, our dark hair and unusual eyes—two different ends of the blue-violet scale—our high foreheads and sharp chins, even our glasses. People in Ausable Forks who didn't even know me would say, "You're Mel Fisher's daughter, aren't you? You have your father's eyes." I said mine were slightly different but deep down I was heritage proud.

Mornings when my father woke up and went immediately to painting, when he bypassed breakfast until ten, I ignored my stomach's loud growls and waited too. If my father wore a red baseball cap, I searched the house for its twin and let it slump over my eyes. Even at fifteen, even in my rebellion, I still lived in this unconscious lean toward my translation of his life.

But the past winter, as my mother flew further from my father's compelling orbit, a change had begun in me too. I was still desperate for our artist bond, but I was more willing to notice truths about my father. As I began to realize how wrong he could be, how his insistence on giving Sam the jackknife had brought us here, a state of confusion fermented inside, promising a less comfortable freedom than adapting to my father's certainty.

Chapter 11

Another weekend arrived. Sam still slept. "You have to see people, Molly," my aunt kept saying. So I decided to go to the Boat House, hang out for an hour, see if Zoe Novato was there and if she even remembered me.

I heard the noise and laughter way before I reached the end of our road, and I almost turned back. Saturday nights, the Boat House drew crowds of townies, lake summer kids, and occasional packs of lanky guys from the state college in Plattsburgh. But I forced myself to walk in.

Zoe was already at the sound board, surrounded by boys I'd never seen.

I stood in the doorway, watching from across the room. She looked just the same. Face down in study, a little smile on her lips, occasionally lifting her eyes to the blond teenager who pointed to this or that, probably giving her instructions. The band was setting up, the drummer trying to get his snare tuned, the bursts of sound causing everyone to shout then quiet when he stopped. Zoe was wearing black jeans and a black T-shirt with the sleeves cut off. She seemed dangerous, not the wholesome person waterskiing behind Chad's motorboat. Not friend material at all, but still I watched her, as if she were a thousand-piece puzzle spread out on a card table, as if she could be fitted into something I could count on this summer. Her facial planes were sharp and defined, with cheekbones rising under her pale eyes and brows as red and untamed as her long hair. But it was her movement I remembered and saw again now—the dancer inside her skin, barely restrained, that made every action graceful.

Sarah lounged against the door to the men's bathroom, blinking at a tall college guy in a Striker T-shirt. I'd seen him before, Mark Something. Sarah's silver navel ring flashed like a grin when she moved her stomach, which she did often and visibly, the tan line of it peeking between a thin top and sparkle-edged low riders. Tonight her hair was gelled back into thick sleekness. Mark obviously appreciated it. At one point, he leaned in and almost took a bite out of her neck. The giggle changed to a laugh you could hear across the room.

I must've moved in reaction, because Sarah looked up and waved brightly, as if I were her best friend. Zoe hadn't seen me yet. She bent farther over the board and the blond guy bent with her, their faces almost touching. I expected her to straighten up and push him away for being a complete jerk, but she turned up her face again, smiling and asking something over another burst of drum. Chad was standing by the bar, looking at Zoe, scowling.

Lester called out, "Let some more flies in why don't cha, we don't have nearly enough."

Everyone turned suddenly. I realized I was still holding the screen door open, but an arms-entwined couple came through and I pretended I was holding it open for them. Zoe sent me a quick smile that created a rush of heat up my neck. I leaned on the wall, gave her a few fingers of wave.

"Figured it out, huh." Chad was beside me. I must've looked startled.

"The door," he said. "The flies."

I sent him a smile of relief. "Been shutting doors since I was a kid. Aren't you playing?"

"Lisa and I aren't getting along. They found someone else for the summer." His face was the fiery red of an afternoon on the boat. "Hey, Zoe skied on the plywood today. You should've seen her."

I forced myself not to sound like I cared that much. "You drive?"

"All afternoon." Chad ran his finger forward and back, forward and back, in the air. "Pretty boring actually. Except for the scenery."

I knew he wasn't talking about the mountains. We both looked over at her. The blond guy had moved on to a group of girls in the far booth and the band's lead singer was talking with Zoe. She pointed at me.

I pushed myself off the wall.

Chad moved forward with me. "How's your brother doing?"

For a minute, I felt the sounds of the room like an ocean, two distinct waves breaking over my head at the same time. Someone bumped me and my backpack slid off my shoulder. I looped it around a couple of fingers, moving toward Zoe, thinking of my brother small and motionless between white sheets. "All right," I said. "It's only been thirteen days."

Chad maneuvered closer, his breath minty with toothpaste. "Hey, I keep wanting to stop in. See him. Do you think that would be Okay?"

We stood a few feet from the sound board, waiting for Zoe to turn toward us. It was bizarre just being here, a place where everyone was partying instead of lying still on thin white sheets. I didn't need anyone forcing me to talk about things I couldn't change. As the noise level grew intense, as the lead guitarist and bass player began riffing, I was washed in a memory of Sammy's room, its deep quiet. I imagined bringing the band over to play in the hall. Maybe it would wake him. Maybe Chad could wake him. I certainly couldn't.

Chad persisted. "How about tomorrow? Zoe doesn't ski on Sundays."

Then there was Zoe. She still hadn't looked at us again. And Chad was nailing me with his eyes, and the conversation was making my tongue feel unnatural, like English was a language I only spoke clumsily.

Sourness rose in my throat, coating my tongue, and I swallowed it down. I commanded Zoe in my mind to throw out her lifeline, to really be my friend. Instead, she leaned on Lisa's arm and gave her a little kiss on the cheek. The singer wrapped the arm around Zoe in a tight hug that made Zoe almost disappear into Lisa's T-shirt.

"You don't have to answer right away," Chad was saying. "I can wait. Let's get you something to drink."

We slid onto stools. Chad pulled out a five. I ordered iced tea, with lemon this time. Lester grinned at me and brought two slices on a paper napkin. I was going to ask him for a plate, but I just squeezed one close to my face, letting the citrus cool my skin. The band had begun playing a loud metal tune, and Chad leaned toward me again.

I shook my head and pointed to the stage. Maybe Lester's lemons were bad. Maybe I had sudden food poisoning.

I picked up one of the used slices and sniffed it.

"Aren't you worried?" Chad said. "I'd be crazy with worry if it was my brother."

"I'm Okay," I said.

Lisa was nuzzling Zoe's hair.

Chad moved closer. "I wanted to tell you about this one dream I had. It was so strange, but awesome too. Sam and I —"

"Shut the fuck up," I said evenly.

"What?" Chad said.

"Hey, Lester," I yelled, "when did you last change your iced tea machine?"

Lester came over, polishing a glass.

"Taste this." I pushed my iced tea toward him. Sharp pain was rocketing my belly now.

Lester sniffed the glass. "Smells Okay."

"Taste it."

Lester tasted it. "Damn dishwasher doesn't rinse right." He reached toward Chad's root beer. "Yours Okay?"

Zoe's arm flashed white across the room and tea boiled up my throat.

The dance floor was packed now. I hopped my way past moving couples, my hand to my mouth. Ducked under flinging arms, heard Zoe call my name, saw Sarah necking seriously outside the men's bathroom. Knocked hard on the women's, rattling the knob.

"It's *occupied*," a voice said, "it's *locked*."

I pushed Sarah and Mark off the door to the men's bathroom, ignoring Mark's "Hey babe," shut the door fast, and let sourness and lemon and a hot dog dinner hit the sink.

It seemed to last five minutes, my body letting it all go. Soon there was nothing more to come up. Nothing except the familiar black guilt that swept up my throat, more stealthily than the vomit, harder to push down. It was full of memories I didn't want: Sammy on the hospital gurney; the sound of my mother crying, her face blotched and red; my father's hands carrying my brother through the doorway marked "Emergency."

I slumped to the floor by the cracked old toilet, letting tears ruin my mascara, slowly seeing the near memories like a terrible family slide show.

The door handle rattled. I heard it over the band's sound blasting into the tiny space, hardly muffled by the pine walls, the lead singer's voice pouring past the closed door, a second voice harmonizing. I grabbed toilet paper, blew my nose and wiped my face, and heaved myself off the floor.

Chad was outside. "Molly? Are you Okay?"

"No," I said. "Zoe has the mike balance totally off."

Chad looked confused then held out a glass. "I got you a Coke." He waved at the air coming from the bathroom. "Whew, that's rank. Let's go outside for a few minutes. Get you some fresh air. You look kind of pale." He took my elbow and gently moved me out of the doorway. I let his kindness fall over me and leaned on his arm a little as we walked past the oblivious Sarah toward the stillness of Cloud Lake.

We sat on the edge of sand and water, where the lake shimmered darkly. It was almost ten, but in the summer north we had long twilights. The mountains rose against the sky, highlighted by stars that were just beginning to peek out.

"My brother was learning the constellations," I said, lying back. The sand felt like a dry cushion, and Chad lay back too. He was humming a little under his breath, following a tune the band was pumping through the open windows. He shifted closer to me. I could feel the heat of skin warmed from a day on the lake.

"He showed me the basic ones, like Orion." I pointed. "Those three stars are his belt. That W is Cassiopeia. The Dippers are over our docks."

"He must be smart," Chad said. One finger absently stroked my arm, so light at first I thought I imagined it. It felt sweet more than electric, so I didn't move.

"My father gave him this astronomy book for Christmas," I said. "Sammy learned everything from the pictures. He was the smartest kid in his first-grade class." Shit, I told myself, what's wrong with you? It's only been thirteen days. "He is the smartest kid."

Chad withdrew his hand and raised himself up on his elbows. His profile was etched against the lake. He was good-looking in a preppy way, streaked brown hair past his ears, a sharp chin and high cheekbones like my mother's. He wore wire-rimmed glasses, like me, but when he drove the boat for Zoe, he wore cool sunglasses on cords.

I spoke to the cheekbones. "*Was* instead of *is*. I don't know why I do that." Tears stung and I blinked, glad of the near dark.

"It's Okay," he said, "you've been through a lot. Maybe we all just need a break from the stress." The lake lapped invisibly at our feet. "Sarah said you used to dance. Ballet or something."

Why was he bringing that up now? "It's been ages. I don't dance anymore."

"Why not?"

I shrugged. "I'm out of shape. And it seems pointless, now."

"You look like you're in great shape." When I didn't answer, Chad put his hand on my arm. It trembled a little, and I had the sudden realization that he liked me. Maybe he thought I liked him. "You haven't given up, have you? With all the waiting, it must be tough."

"Nobody's given up," I said sharply. Someone was out twilight fishing and I could see an occasional flash of yellow light along the shoreline. I thought about my father who fished every spring in the Ausable, with his thigh boots and waders to ward off the cold. Nobody from around here gave up anything that easy.

"I know you haven't. I don't know why I said that." He sat up. "Do you want to go in now?"

I nodded.

Chad got to his feet, fluid, and brushed off sand, not looking at me. We were halfway to the Boat House door when he said, like it had just occurred to him, "If I asked you to dance, would you say yes?"

I just stood there. "What?"

"You know, move to music." Chad held the screen door open for me. He moved his hips a little, grinning. "Lots of people do it."

Chad Anderson was flirting with me. He was asking me to dance. Like a date. I couldn't speak.

"When you get things sorted out with Zoe," he said, "I'll be waiting."

The drummer gave a flourish of cymbals and the song ended. Dancers clapped sporadically. I could see Zoe get up, turn toward the bar, find me. She beckoned.

I moved slowly through the thirsty dancers as another song started. When I reached the sound board table, she was leaning against it, watching me, arms crossed.

"Sarah said you were going to help," she shouted. "Be my right-hand girl or something." She sounded annoyed. "But instead you're hanging out on the beach."

I felt my face flush. "Sarah never asked me to help. I was actually throwing up. And thanks, I'm Okay now."

"Sorry," she said. She stuck her hands in her jeans pockets, looking less confident, leaned closer so I could hear her. "I just haven't got the hang of this board, and Sarah said you'd been doing it all summer."

I looked at the angles of her thin wrists protruding from

denim. I forced my eyes to the sliders. "You've got the mike balances pretty screwy. Didn't that skanky lead singer give you any tips?" Lisa was almost offstage, playing a riff for a girl I knew from school who was dancing on the floor in front of the band.

"Lisa's so stoned I didn't get half of what she said." Zoe was looking at me like she found every word I said unique and fascinating. "Were you really throwing up?"

"It's all right. I'm fine now. A momentary lapse."

"Something Lester made?"

I shook my head, letting it rock for a minute, back and forth, keeping time with the band's song. *Nobody's giving up*, I whispered in time with the music. Nobody ever will.

The song ended. Zoe and I became an island again. Around us were a hundred voices all talking at once, little shrieks from girls greeting each other and the deep voices of senior boys trying to score. The drummer was now tightening his cymbals, the tinny clashes mingling with the voices and laughter. It was familiar, yet I couldn't hear any of it. Zoe smelled like lake water. I watched her fingers stroke the black plastic parts of the board.

"I thought we were going to be good friends," she said, almost too low to hear. "Will you sit here? Please? Show me what to do?"

There was only one chair at the table. She moved quickly away, pulled a chair out from under a big guy who was about to sit down. He caught himself in time and was as dazed by Zoe as everyone, nodding at her, letting himself become chairless in sacrifice to that smile. She slid the chair behind me. "I'll get us something to drink," she said. "You'll be thirsty by now. Sit."

I sat.

Chad passed by, nodding at me. "Don't forget the dance," he said.

Zoe looked at me, her eyes interested. "I didn't know you liked to dance."

Chapter 12

Five summers before, when I was ten, my parents sent me to camp in Lake George to be with my cousin Sarah. We were all in White Hawk cabin that year. Sarah's best friend was a girl named Chloe.

Chloe had dark curls she brushed for fifteen minutes every night, and her voice was low like a boy's. Her small face was easily hidden in the mass of hair. The orange crate beside her bed was stacked with interesting books. Sarah told me Chloe's family was dirt poor, her father had left them one night, the family lived in a Baltimore row house, and Chloe had tried smoking. I thought she was the most intriguing, mysterious person I'd ever seen.

I was passionate about ballet when I was ten. Chloe took lessons too. We practiced barre exercises on the porch railing, ignoring Sarah's jealousy and anyone who made fun of us.

One evening Chloe said to meet her in the living room about a half hour before we were supposed to be in bed. I asked if Sarah would be there.

"Just us," Chloe said, and cannonballed off the dock.

I waited in the living room that night until nine. There was a mattress couch, covered with Indian print bedspreads and fat ratty pillows, set up on cement blocks near the fireplace. Someone had left the fire going, a slow log burning red in the darkness. The little kids were already in their cabins, and the counselors were making the rounds with their big flashlights, counting heads. I sat alone on the mattress couch, my knees pulled up to my chest, my arms around them, waiting.

As it got closer to the hour I would be counted missing if I wasn't a lump on a lumpy mattress. I remembered our earlier talk . . . About Chloe's boredom with boys, how one of her books said girls could be more than friends. It didn't hurt anybody, she said. Did I want to try? I wanted to be regarded as someone who would try. Although at age ten I couldn't imagine what she was talking about.

The counselor on duty passed through the living room on her way to check my cabin. She saw me, casually mentioned that it was almost nine, and she would see me at White Hawk in a few minutes, yes? I unfolded my legs and got off the couch to walk there, stopping at the girls' bathroom to brush my teeth and pee. The cabin was full, all the beds full of sleepy and chattering bunkmates. As I passed Chloe's bed I saw her black hair on the white pillowcase, blankets pulled over her face. I put on my nightgown, hating the itchy lace collar, and got into my cold sheets, huddled into myself, glad of what had not happened.

The next morning I saw Chloe in the dining room at breakfast, laughing her low laugh with Sarah as they waited for toast. She said hi to me, not really looking at me at first then staring into my eyes, no embarrassment, no shame.

"I fell asleep," she said.

"Me, too." I smiled at her, relieved.

Sarah looked at us, questioning. "So?"

Things went on as before.

Chapter 13

July 4 came and went. I hadn't seen Zoe again, but I noticed her out on the lake with Chad almost every morning. My father, my mother and I watched fireworks from the dock, but I missed Sammy's sweeping fistfuls of sparklers against the dark air. I couldn't even stay to the grand finale.

In books people lost love, homes, jobs and families. They mourned and moved on. Loss was about endings. My loss was endless. Waiting, hoping and not knowing dulled my days and nights, waking me up from dark watery dreams.

Anna came over a few evenings, to talk with my mother and cheer me up. I pretended I was asleep so I didn't have to say hello. Usually it was still light, plenty of evening left, but I wanted to be alone. One evening Anna didn't even knock, just came in and called for my mother.

"I'm here," my mother called back. "I'm just going out."

"Someplace fun?" I could hear Anna settle onto our creaky wicker couch.

"I really don't know if it'll be fun." My mother was in the

kitchen, rattling dishes.

"Are you taking the plane up?"

"I wouldn't be able to enjoy flying tonight." I could hear her wistfulness. My mother loved flying in the late summer evenings, swooping over the green sides of the mountains and the blue lakes.

"I thought you liked flying when it's wild."

"I'm not a total fool."

"I don't think you're any kind of fool." My aunt shuffled around the room, picking something up, putting it down. "Did you like that lamp I brought over? I have another one in the car. They are just dirt cheap."

"I need to get out of here for a while."

"Where's Molly?" Anna said.

"Sleeping. On her porch."

Her voice lowered but I could still make out the words. "I know it's been a terrible pressure cooker, all those days at the hospital, nothing to do but wait."

My mother's voice was rising. "I don't know if I can take it much longer."

"Sam will wake up."

"That's what I keep telling myself, but God, I don't know. Why did this have to happen right now?" My mother laughed, a bitter sound. "I reconcile myself to stay and work it out, be a good person, and this happens to make sure."

Chills rushed over me. For years, I had lived with the suspicion of my mother's imminent departure from our lives. Some afternoons this past winter, when the fights got particularly bad, I would come home from school and go straight to the kitchen, looking for the note. Sometimes there would be a note, but the worst it said was that she would be staying with Anna for a few days and could I please look after Sammy.

"Melvin loves you like the sun and moon."

My mother sighed, quiet and terrible. "Do you realize how much of a prison that kind of love can be?"

I watched her a lot after that. I went with her to see my

brother as often as I could but my throat grew choked with guilt each visit. What did it matter, anyway, if my mother might leave as soon as Sam got well? Both my parents cared more about Sam than me. I could slip into invisibility without notice. And that's what I tried to do.

But there were occasional mornings, that first week of July, when waking alone, I forgot to instantly feel bad. Some days my dreams wouldn't always contain memories of the boat turning slowly, the water at dawn, reeds wrapped around a small leg, Sammy's bruised wrist. I would hear my mother's off-key tune from the kitchen and tell myself she'd changed her mind. Then I'd catch her sitting on the porch too, staring at trees, within a stillness so unlike her.

Once we passed each other at midnight in the hall, and she gasped and knocked against a little table, scaring us both. She carried on for a few minutes about how noisy she was. Eventually I had to lead her back to bed.

My father was a darker presence in the house, chopping wood, painting fiercely. Each evening he visited Sammy, sometimes staying overnight, sometimes returning to his studio and staying there until two or three. I would hear his feet on the porch, the creak of the bed when he lay down. The silence of his breathing.

The heat grew dense in the air around my skin and my body felt laden with a hundred weights. My scraggly hair grew long enough to tame in two short braids which kept it off my face.

Zoe and Sam became intricately linked in my heart during those July days. I remembered Sammy's soft cheek and the imagined softness of Zoe's Indian Paintbrush hair. Sometimes in my dreams, Zoe would be in the boat and she'd turn before Sammy fell.

When I opened *Anna Karenina* just to be in another country, it was increasingly hard to read about dying by choice. I grew used to just sitting quietly in the hospital chair, watching my mother page through her mystery, watching her pace the room, listening to Sammy breathe, willing my mother to get up and go down the hall for coffee, for anything, just so I could have five minutes alone with my brother. But she didn't leave very often. So I just followed his breathing with my own, saying *I'm sorry* over and over under my breath.

Often, when I was alone in the cabin, I'd catch myself listening. It wasn't until a few days passed that I realized I was listening for echoes of my brother's voice, the way he sang to me through the floorboards, cool and sweet. Once, when I was taking a shower, letting the steam pummel shoulders sore from stacking wood, I swore I heard him. His voice was so certain in my ears, I quickly turned off the water and stood still. "Hello?" I called to the empty building. Then, "Sammy?" in a whisper. Outside a mourning dove hoo-hoo'ed and the shower dripped alongside my ear. All else was silent.

The one normal person I spoke to regularly was my Aunt Anna. She called to badger me about getting fresh air, came by with groceries and jokes and town gossip, planted a line of straggling marigolds in junk store pots on our porch, set inspiring used books by my bed. Sitting on the dock, reading, I watched Chad Anderson driving for Zoe. Chad waved to me when they passed. Zoe was focused on her skiing, but sometimes she'd wave too.

When Sarah's new boyfriend Mark began doing sound for Lisa's band, I started seeing a lot of Sarah. I thought it might get me closer to Zoe, and Mark told me I had a good ear. So they asked me to come along whenever the band played in Plattsburgh or Saranac.

Sarah was full of dating opportunities for me. She said I needed distraction. And I began to almost welcome it.

Like her mother but with much less grace, Sarah wanted to cheer me up and kept pointing me toward Chad. But other than two fast dances the night I threw up at the Boat House, I hadn't seen him closer than across the blue expanse of lake.

Zoe, the person I wanted most to see close up, hadn't invited me to do anything fun.

Chapter 14

The fourth week after the accident, the July heat was constant, pressing all of us flat. I got up at five one evening, after a nap, knowing I'd be back late. I was trying out Aunt Anna's idea to get out more and Sarah had asked me to help with sound again, a concert in nearby Saranac.

When I wandered bleary-eyed to the kitchen, my mother was heating milk for coffee. Her travel mug was on the counter.

I felt a tingle of alarm. "Why are you home? Did something happen?"

My mother turned off the burner and poured hot milk into the travel mug. "Your father and I switched shifts. I'm going in for a few hours tonight. Do you want to keep me company?"

I thought of Sarah pleading on the phone earlier, reluctantly shook my head. "I'm going out."

"Good. You need to get out." The mug clicked shut. "Who's driving?"

"Sarah."

She reached across the table, gathering a book that sat near my cereal bowl. "I'm glad you finally found a friend for the summer, honey. You're by yourself way too much."

Sarah and I were far from friends. It was more a matter of frequency and mutual need. I chewed slowly, granola loud in my ears.

My mother picked up a bookmark and stuck it carefully into the pages. "I'm just happy you're not sitting in your room, reading. Or painting by yourself all day."

How do you know what I'm doing all day? I wanted to yell. I tried to finish my cereal, ignoring the way her shoulders looked incredibly thin, hunched like an old person's inside her summer sweater. I took my bowl to the sink, began to walk out of the kitchen. Her voice stopped me.

"What kind of birthday cake do you want this year?"

I turned, slow. "My birthday isn't for a month, Mom."

"I know." She was opening and shutting her hand, staring at her own fingers like they were foreign objects. "Anna just called. The bakery in Saranac has been trying to deliver a chocolate cake with chocolate icing. For weeks, I guess. I forgot to cancel the order."

"Oh," I said.

"Maybe you want the same kind?"

"That's fine."

My mother had begun washing my cereal bowl. The suncatcher swayed against the open screen, scattering sprinkles of light across her hair. She suddenly bent over at the waist, as if she were diving into the sink.

I moved fast, grabbing her by the arms, lifting her back in place. "Come sit," I said.

She was shaking her head, back and forth, the same stubborn drumbeat my brother used. "Sammy really loved chocolate cake."

"Sammy still does," I said.

She smiled a little at her book, her travel mug still waiting on the table. "I guess I better get going."

"Do you want me to come with you?"

"No, you go on. Have some fun."

But neither of us moved.

On the shelf above the table were two of my father's sketches of Sammy. He had affixed them to foam core so they leaned straight and bright against the honey-colored wood. My mother was staring at the sketches as if they made her sadder than anything else could. I felt the air in the room like a live thing, heavy and breathing with our family's sorrow.

"Your father thought you'd want to see those, since you were painting so much now."

There was a little twitch in my chest, the unexpectedness of my father's kindness toward me. "They're really good, aren't they," I said.

"Better than anything he's ever done of Sammy," my mother said. "Your father could never get Sammy to stay still enough before."

The image came of one January afternoon, finding my mother asleep on the couch in front of our wood stove, her face pink with heat and dreams. I had gotten a hand mirror from my bedroom and sat on the floor near her, held the mirror up so I could study both our faces. We were so different on the outside, she lean and pale and ethereal, me rosy and sturdy. She was equally beautiful in sleep and despair, and I could never be.

I walked my mother up to her car then went over to my father's studio. When he was at the hospital, the door was always unlocked now. I took two twenty-dollar bills from his desk drawer and put them in my jeans pocket. I borrowed it for Cokes and snacks. When I asked my father a certain way, he'd always give it to me, but it grew easier just to take it without asking.

On my way out I went over to the table by the window. There was a half-finished sketch of Sammy's hands, his new bear clasped against the white sheet.

Even though two of the sketches had come to live in the main cabin, many more lined the studio table. Totally unlike his portraits of women, these were much less detailed but with a kindness in every line. A face that was unremarkable in line at Price Chopper on a snowy morning, under my father's fingers became softer at the edges, the expression illuminated in a way I couldn't yet define.

I knew it was my father's rescue attempt. I studied every line, trying to understand how he could love Sammy that much and never show it any other way.

Chapter 15

Chad had been the one to really rescue my brother—and all of us—that June morning on the lake. He had been on his Jet Ski, watching when Sam fell overboard. And as my boat bumped over its own wake, speeding back toward the far shore to look for Sammy, Chad had turned too, the Jet Ski sliding, the two wakes crossing as we moved along the lightening expanse of lake.

I remember he was always slightly ahead of me. We were both facing the rising sun—and the water and sky, the boat's metal runners, the crystalline white wake, all felt harsh in the new light.

Chad had circled the Jet Ski, narrowing around a spot about twenty feet from the still-dark line of trees along the uninhabited shore. He tossed his sunglasses on the console and jumped in, treading in a circle.

"There!" I could see a bright pink flip-flop resting on the water, bobbing in the receding wake. I pointed frantically.

And Chad swam. He was a proud swimmer. Last summer, he had circled the lake, five or six miles, his father rowing patiently in a boat beside him, the echo of their transistor radio letting everyone know the great feat. His arms flashed white against the dark water, toward my brother somewhere beneath the surface. Then he dove.

I jumped in too, not remembering my glasses until I felt the pain of plastic against my nose. June lakes are almost freezing; it takes your breath, but I felt nothing.

Chad surfaced, a few feet from me. "I see something. Going down again." He took a huge breath and pushed under. I followed.

The lake was murky here, but I saw something too, paler than the rocks. Chad grabbed out, missing, surfacing, then moving down again. I felt my throat burn and some part of me went on alert, realizing I had run out of air. When I reached the surface, I inhaled as deeply as I could, held my glasses tighter against my nose, and sank again.

Chad had Sammy's arm and he was pulling hard. My brother's face was distorted through the stirred-up water, his legs still captured by rocks and weeds.

I swam closer, using one hand, reaching for Sammy's other arm, and we both tugged for a minute, but Sammy's foot or leg or some lower part of him was lodged.

Use both hands, I realized.

I reached down.

Between the two of us, we got Sammy to the surface and turned him on his back. I treaded water, shivering, pleading, "Sammy, wake up. Wake up."

But Chad Anderson pushed me aside and I went under for a second. When I came up, he was cradling Sammy's head, pinching Sammy's nose, starting CPR. That's when Sammy finally moved. He coughed once and jerked, spitting.

"Okay," Chad said. The sun was lighting the water so fiercely, I had to squint to see him. My legs, my arms were so tired. "We've got to get him back to shore now, fast. He may have hit his head." He was already swimming to the Jet Ski.

He's my brother, I thought. "Put him in the boat," I screamed.

"No," Chad said, his voice stern. "I can get there faster."

When we got to the dock, I leaned on the boat horn. I remember how the sound blasted through the morning quiet, how the crows rose from the cedars in black clouds. How I leaned again, again, again, then began screaming for my dad.

My father ran out of the cabin, still in his sweats. "What's happening?"

I pointed up the hill. "Sammy," I said. "It's Sammy."

Chapter 16

When Sarah picked me up for the Saranac concert, she handed me a tiny green package. I knew what it was: a condom. I read the package in the light from the dash. *Extra sensitive.*

"I don't exactly need this," I said.

My cousin gunned the car and we sped down the driveway, bouncing over potholes. "Chad might."

"Then give it to Chad." I tried to stuff the condom into her purse which lay on the seat between us but she pushed my hand away.

"Chad thinks you're totally interesting. He told me."

"Chad Anderson rescued Sammy," I said, flushing. "End of story."

"Chad," Sarah enunciated the name like a game show host introducing promising contestants, "wants to get in your pants. And you're blind not to see it."

I didn't say anything.

Sarah lit a cigarette. We skimmed down the darkening road.

"How's Sammy?" she said.

"He's Okay. Why are you doing this?"

"Doing what?"

"Pushing me on Chad Anderson."

"Because," she blew smoke out her window, "you need cheering up. Something to take your mind off things. Because there's an art and science to men, and I'm doing my best to teach you, since you are obviously not educated whatsoever."

Pines rushed past.

"I asked Chad to meet us there," Sarah added.

"Jesus." I slid lower in my seat. The car's lights swung up the hill past the Boat House. "He's going to think I'm the worst jerk in the world."

My cousin nodded. "That's why you need me."

Mark's brother led us to a card table set up by the stage. Lisa was stomping around onstage. She waved to us. Sarah sat at the card table, studying the board. I stood awkwardly beside her chair, getting used to the dim light, wondering if Zoe would be there helping too.

I was about to ask when I heard Chad's voice.

"You working tonight?"

He wore some cologne that smelled spicy and nice; his jacket was tan and his jeans pressed, like he was going on a date.

I couldn't look at him very long, thinking about the condom in my pocket. "I wouldn't call it working. I don't really know what I'm doing."

"You know a lot more than me. Or Zoe."

"Is Zoe here?" I asked, as casually as I could. Zoe's name had caused a prickly flush on my chest. I felt it racing up my neck and I yanked up my scoop top to cover as much skin as I could.

Lisa strode toward us, her lace tights and high boots catching the light.

"Hey," she said to me, ignoring Chad. "When's our sound check?"

"Ask Sarah," I said. "I just help."

She bent to pull a coiled cord from a duffel bag on the floor next to the table. "Where's your friend tonight? I was hoping to dance with her again."

I stood, mute. This was getting to be too much. She looped the cord over her shoulder and looked up at me.

I nudged Sarah. "Lisa wants to know about the sound check."

Mark was there, leaning over Sarah's neck, breathing hard in her ear. She swatted him away. "This setup's for shit, Mark."

"Complaints go to the management." Mark smiled at Lisa. "Sound check's in thirty minutes."

Lisa grinned back and moved toward the stage, the silky red fringe on her skirt swaying as she walked. I watched Mark watch her.

"Thirty minutes is pushing it," Sarah said. "Go get that brother of yours, tell him to get his ass over here and help me."

"What can I do?" I asked, not really wanting to do anything.

Chad took my arm. "Come get ice cream with me. Sarah will let us know when she needs us."

Chad pulled me down the block toward the flickering Carvel sign. A kid Sammy's age was eating a chocolate cone, getting it all over his face. Tiny dark waves lapped Lake Flower's beach, and wind wrapped my bare legs.

"It's way too chilly for ice cream," I said. It was. "We should go back."

"It's summer," Chad said. "And I've got a new CD in my car. I want you to eat ice cream with me and listen to it."

Beach sand skittered across the tarmac. The wind was making me really shiver. "I get my learner's next month," I said. "When I turn sixteen."

"What kind do you want?"

I ordered pistachio. "Let's go hear that CD," Chad said, putting an arm around me, biting into his cone. He steered me back toward the parking lot.

Several new cars were crammed into the spaces. I didn't even know if Zoe drove. She was older than me, about Chad's age, so she probably did. I slipped my cone into a trashcan when Chad wasn't looking, stuck my fists in my pockets to warm my hands. My fingers touched the smooth packet of the condom. I tried folding it into a tiny ball but the ring edge was stiff.

The car door opened with a tug. We got in. Chad craned forward, fiddling with controls in the glove compartment. After a few seconds, he leaned back. Violins and cello began to sweep over us, the same complicated music my father listened to when he painted.

"Yo Yo Ma," Chad said. He turned up the volume until the cello was rubbing my skin. "Awesome cellist," he mouthed in my ear. I nodded, moving away from his leg hot against me. But his arm lifted to settle on the back of my seat, encircling my shoulders, and I gave in.

The melody became tender, softer. It filled the car and I grew even stiller, feeling my body receive each note in its wounded places. The sound erased Sarah and Lisa, the sound board, the band playing boring tunes inside the hall. My mother's impending flight. Even Zoe. Slowly, almost imperceptibly it even began to ease the constant burn about Sammy, and my lungs released a grip that had been around them for weeks.

I closed my eyes, letting the memory of that day wash over me, familiar in all its details, grooved in my mind from daily tracings. The sun on the water, the air soft on my face, the dark shadowed shore of Dougall Mountain. How I'd swung the wheel and arced the boat, showing off my driving skills, listening for Sammy's laugh. The pain was still there, but more like a dull ache than a deep puncture.

We sat quiet as the music ended. I was a little dazed. The CD player clicked and Chad leaned forward to shut it off.

"That was amazing."

Chad ran his hand along my shoulder. "I knew you'd like it."

Like wasn't quite the word. But I nodded in the dark.

"Molly," Chad said after a minute, "I have to tell you something." He shuffled his feet, not easy in the tiny car. "I ran out of air," he said, blowing out a breath. His arm came so tightly around my shoulders it hurt. "I knew I should go right back down and get Sammy. But I had this little cramp in my leg. I waited a few seconds. Too long, I think."

Inside, the band had quieted. Waves from the lake pounded

loud in the distance.

"Even three seconds can make a lot of difference in coma victims. This could be all my fault."

"It's not all your fault."

"I can't sleep." He said this apologetically. "It must be."

My leg suddenly cramped. I tried to stretch it out, but there was no room. The smell of Chad's cologne was suffocating me but my window refused to roll down. I jerked at the handle. "This is stuck."

Chad reached over and cranked it. "Do you think I need to tell Sammy?"

"Why are you asking me?" I stuck my face out the window toward the lake breeze, gulped air.

"I've waited weeks. For you to say yes. I don't want to go see him if you don't want me to. It has to be Okay with you."

"Why?"

"Because of all we've been through," he said, "together."

There was a meaningful pause.

"I don't care," I said. "You could've gone to see him anytime. We can go tomorrow." I tried to take the words back then swallowed hard, attempting kindness. "I know he'd want to see you."

"Excellent." Chad sounded relieved. "I'll see if I can get the car."

The door to the community center burst open, and we heard Lisa's high laugh. "They're on break." I quickly rolled up the window. "Sarah will need me."

"You're a super girl, Molly," Chad said. He reached over and turned my chin until I was facing him. Then he kissed me, just a tiny kiss, on the lips.

Chapter 17

Sarah would've been proud of me. It looked like I had a boyfriend for sure. I didn't feel at all excited.

When we went back into the hall, Zoe wasn't there. Disappointment made me so dizzy I could only help a little with the sound board. I mostly sat in a corner and collected Chad's invitations to dance. Around midnight, Sarah and Mark took me home. They dropped me off in the parking field, where I said goodnight and used my flashlight to navigate the path toward the cabin.

No lights were on, so I continued down to the dock. I wanted to look at the stars for a while before I went to bed.

The air was warmer here, very still, wrapped in an envelope of new summer heat. The path rose toward my flashlight beam in spurts, disappeared into dark behind me. The dock boards were still warm from the sun. I balled up my sweater for a cushion and sat, my legs crossed. The water lapped against the dock supports and boulders lining the shore. As if on cue, a pair of loons began calling to each other, one across the lake and one not far from where I sat. That summer there were at least two pairs nesting, their warbles and shrill calls strangely comforting. From my bed on the cabin's lakeside sleeping porch, I often listened to them in the depths of night. I always imagined them finding each other, even in the dark.

At one point I closed my eyes to listen, and the lake smell rose to meet me, sweet and weedy. The night was late and the breeze felt like silk against my face. I felt safe and undisturbed, and eventually I began to dream.

The sharp crack of a stick woke me. I heard footsteps on the path. A flashlight was moving jerkily, as if held by someone who didn't really know her way. I got to my feet slowly and carefully, thinking about where to hide. The trees were big enough, but grass and leaves would rustle and give me away. And by now the person had seen my shape on the dock. So I just held my unlit flashlight against my chest like a weapon and stood, waiting.

"I thought you'd be down here." Zoe turned off her light and stepped onto the dock. My breath hitched in shock. She stopped a few feet from me, and I could tell by the dark outline of her profile against the lake that she was looking up. "God bless it," she said softly. "Is it always like this?"

I looked up too.

About a million stars swam above us. I could see the Dippers. Orion's belt. I sank down on the dock, Zoe as close to me as she had been in the boat, giving me zero room to move over, but I was glad for the warmth of her leg, inches away. It didn't burn like Chad's leg but somehow felt comfortably like my own. Like there was nothing unusual about meeting here at this hour.

When Zoe spoke, her voice was gentler, awed by the stars. "I looked for you at the Boat House tonight." I turned toward her, surprised. Her head was still tilted back. "I was there for hours. You never came."

"Sarah took me to Saranac for a concert. She needed my help."

"You could've told me."

I felt a thrill. "Why?"

"Why not?" Zoe cleared her throat, and the sound echoed off the rocks. "I thought we were getting to know each other."

I thought about this. What had she done to get to know me, except take me out in the boat that day and ask me to help her at the sound board one evening? To my disgust, I'd seen more of Sarah than I had Zoe. I stared across the lake, thinking about what "getting to know each other" might mean to Zoe, and if maybe there was more she wanted. Then there was Sammy. How much had she really heard? Had Chad told her details of my stupidity piloting the boat? I shifted in embarrassment, but she was still talking.

"But we haven't had much of a chance, have we? And when you didn't ask me to ski again, after you were so interested. . . ."

"I hurt my knee, remember. It takes a while to heal."

"Your knee."

"It was just bad timing," I said. "I want to ski with you."

"I see Chad Anderson more than I see you," she said. So do I, I thought. "I thought we were going to be good friends."

"You seem to have plenty of friends," I said. I knew I sounded jealous, but I didn't care. I was jealous. "Plenty of guys at the Boat House drooling over you when you work the board." Especially the night I threw up, I almost said, then decided it wasn't necessary to be that time-specific.

"Guys don't count." She said it like it was a fact. "I want to know, are you interested?"

"What?"

"In getting to know each other."

Above us the Big Dipper poured into nothingness. I took deep breaths like I had in the boat, feeling every bit in danger as I had then. I counted the stars in the Dipper's outline. But each pinpoint of light pressed on my brain. I closed my eyes again and sat there in the balmy dark, listening to the lake lap around Zoe's breathing.

"Maybe you don't want to be friends," she said when I didn't answer. "Maybe you're busy with everyone else, with Chad and Sarah and your family. Chad sure likes you. Is he your boyfriend?"

I thought of the condom still in my pocket. "I don't have a boyfriend," I said, even though hours earlier I'd thought differently.

"Do you want one?"

I shrugged.

"Have you ever been kissed?" she persisted.

What was she driving at? "Of course I've been kissed," I snapped. "Everyone has."

"Well, did you want more than a kiss? Or was it, you know, boring?"

Zoe said *boring* as if she had been kissed more times than she could count, as if anyone with any experience in these matters would understand the difference between a boring kiss and one that was not. I tried to remember Chad's brief alighting of lips on mine. Was it boring? The rush of the music, how I felt hearing it in the car, came back. I tried to remember the lips. I could feel Zoe looking at me.

"I don't know if it was boring," I said, watching the etch of dark mountain against sky. "I don't have much to compare it to."

"That can be a good thing," she said. She paused, then spoke to the stars. "Have you ever kissed a girl?"

I made my voice indignant, outraged, what I hoped was good cover. "Not likely." I stood up in a fluid motion that only succeeded in knocking my flashlight into the water.

"Not likely," Zoe said. She was smiling, I could hear it in her voice.

"Why the hell did you ask me that?" The anger felt real now, focused in a beam. I sent it past her into the dark lake. If only I had turned on my flashlight when she came down the path, I would at least see it shining up from the bottom now.

"Why do you think?"

"I'm supposed to be a mind reader?" I tried to stalk past her but was halted where the edge of the dock leapt onto land, tricky footing in the pitch black of a moonless night. I shuffled with one foot on the first flat rock until the rock moved.

"You maybe need to borrow my flashlight?" Zoe asked.

"No," I said. "Thank you." But I didn't move, just stood there, tears starting, keeping my head down in case she decided to shine her light in my face.

Zoe moved forward, took my elbow very gently. Her flashlight was a mammoth lantern from Lowe's and the beam shot out for miles. Anyone could see us practically holding hands on my parents' dock.

I pulled my arm away. "I can walk."

"Whatever." She strode past me across the treacherous rocks, stepping onto stable ground, her flashlight beam aiming up the hill, waiting for me to follow. I walked at the bobbing edge of her circle of light, and we reached the cabin without breaking anything. One lamp shone in the kitchen, lonely after all the stars.

Zoe turned off the flashlight and we stood close in the half-dark. Around us were the usual Adirondack night sounds, an occasional sweep of breeze, the long shapes of the pines circling the clearing in front of the steps. I could hear her breathing.

"Should I come in?"

"My parents are asleep." This was probably a lie, since my mother didn't often sleep and my father didn't often come to bed at all. But I didn't want to risk meeting them.

"I'm practicing tomorrow morning," Zoe said, her voice hesitant. "You don't have to ski, but do you want to watch? I'm trying the plywood."

I'd been jealous when Chad mentioned the plywood circle, watching Zoe ski on it without any bindings, just bare soles balancing on wet wood. What did she think, that I was just one more member of the Zoe Novato Fan Club, that I had nothing better to do than watch her move across water? I had a lot of reading to do for Advanced English. I couldn't just hang around, waiting for her. She wasn't that hot. Even if she could dance better than anyone.

"Please?"

Her voice sounded little, pleading now, like it really mattered if I came to watch, like she really didn't have anyone else. She put a hand on my arm and I moved away sharply, startled by the warmth.

"I thought you were my friend," she said.

It was all so confusing, and my head was swirling in the night air, so I did the easiest thing I could. "Okay," I said. "I guess I have time tomorrow." I opened my mouth to tell her about Sammy, warn her of the risks of being my friend, but she began to move away.

"Ten at the dock. You can bring those cool egg salad sandwiches again, and this time share them." She leaned back for a minute, rocked against my shoulder, the touch friendly, brief, then disappeared up the path, the lantern's forest-sweeping beam fading as she reached the parking area.

Chapter 18

That night, I dreamed of forests in winter.

It was February, the snow packed hard and deep, and my brother and I were snowshoeing on the Bluffs trail that ran above our farmhouse. In the dream we two raced like boats on a white ocean, he turning back to look at me, laughing, calling to the cardinals that alighted bright red against the laden trees. I stopped to fix a loose binding, led him home when he got tired.

It came the night after I met Zoe on the dock, and maybe that's what turned the dream. Because suddenly Sammy and I were lost in the white woods. And although I called out to them, my mother and father were nowhere around.

We floated along silently, our snowshoes leaving pressed patterns behind us. Soon everything was colorless, no birds called, no sun glinted through the laden pines. But Sammy seemed to know where he was going. Every now and then something shiny appeared in his hands, flashing like a beacon.

I always followed.

I lay by the lake the next morning, the dream still with me. It had kept me from sleeping the rest of the night, so I dozed in the sun to the bump of my father's Chris Craft and the slurp of water against the dock, familiar. The boat engine hummed across the lake, and I waited for them to approach.

The night had been hot, and the morning was already scorching. July sun cooked my scalp where my hair parted. I finally draped my T-shirt over my braids and my towel over my feet, lathered on the sunblock, but I could feel the thin lines of burn growing on any uncovered surface.

Zoe zipped back and forth across the water as if she had all the energy in the world, waving to me each time she passed the dock. Chad was driving, in a billowy T-shirt and the cool sunglasses. I felt a thrill each time Zoe lifted her hand toward me, although the thrill was laced with unwanted ideas that wouldn't leave me alone. I thought of the one gay girl in our class, how she looked so different than Zoe, how she crept along hallways as close to the wall as possible. Nobody sat with her at lunch. When I found myself wondering how Zoe's lips would compare to Chad's, I picked up my book.

Every now and then I roused myself, watched as Zoe stood up on the plywood circle and shimmied past, over and over. I couldn't resist pushing my glasses tighter against my nose, trying to see her face. Sometimes I could catch her eyes serious with concentration. Sometimes she was smiling into the wind, looking at me, red hair streaming out behind her.

Each time the disc skidded out from under her, as it always did eventually, she let go of the towrope, sank gracefully, and lay on her back, waiting. Chad circled the boat, helped her grab the floating rope handle. Bursts of laughter drifted across the expanse of lake between us, and I wondered what was so funny about falling.

I had made the egg salad. But nobody stopped to eat the sandwiches, so I had one, then the other two, myself. By noon, when it was way too hot to be on the dock, I gathered my towel and book and sandwich wrappers to find someplace cooler.

As if she knew her audience was leaving, Zoe made big circles close to the dock.

"Molly, where are you going?" she called.

I just smiled and kept gathering my stuff. So what if I was waiting for her to say, "I want you to stay, you of all people, I want you to see this." She wouldn't do that.

But on the last circle, as I was stepping off the dock toward the cabin, I heard her long whistle. I turned in time to see her let go of the rope just after she passed me.

For long moments, she stood suspended on the surface, grinning at me like someone who could save us all.

Chapter 19

Chad's brother's car idled at the end of our dirt road, shiny in the late sun. I climbed in, noticing Chad's creased khaki pants and white shirt. He had set the cool sunglasses on the dash, even wet his hair. It lay flat and dark on his scalp.

"I thought we were meeting at five." He didn't look at me as he spoke, just put the car in first gear and moved off before I even closed the door, like being ten minutes late was a big crime.

"I fell asleep, Okay? Then I had to write a note for my mother." My voice was grumpy but I didn't care. I probably wouldn't have time to get another stuffed animal, and the thought of that almost sent me into a mild panic. If I didn't have something soft to appeal to my brother's hands, for him to clasp against his chest, would he even hear me? I held on as we bumped over a series of potholes and Chad's sunglasses slid into his lap.

He folded them over the visor. "I thought you said your parents didn't care where you went."

"They don't." This wasn't entirely true, but I didn't feel like explaining myself. The nap had left me unsettled.

We reached the main road, and Chad accelerated. The movement forced my head back against the headrest and I let it lie there, watched the telephone wires swing by the road, inhaling then exhaling against the sky. "My mother wants to know when I'll be back, who's driving."

Chad turned onto Route 3. "Did you tell her you were going to see Sam?"

"Course not."

"Why not?"

"I don't know."

I turned my head just enough to see him. It was easier looking at him than talking with him. "You're really dressed up. Didn't you drive for Zoe all day?"

"I'm supposed to be your family, aren't I? If someone at the hospital asks?"

I'd thought he dressed up for Sammy. But I didn't say that.

It was a beautiful afternoon, going into a beautiful evening, and I let the milder heat of the sun soothe my closed eyes. Chad fiddled with the stereo and found a radio station from Plattsburgh. We listened for a while.

"Can we hear that CD again?" I asked.

"What CD?"

"The Yo Yo one. You played it last night." I couldn't believe it had just been last night.

"It's still in the glove compartment."

I fished it out and slid it into the player. The music filled the small space, just as beautiful as the night before. The case said *The Cello Suites.* "Sammy would like this."

"He likes classical?"

"He's pretty advanced musically."

Chad turned into the hospital parking lot. "I can play it for him. I have it on my iPod."

I'd never even thought of playing music for my sleeping brother. It was a good idea. Maybe it would remind him of the million reasons to wake up and join us. "Do you think the nurses will let us?"

"They'd better." Chad looked at me, serious, like we were on a secret mission together.

The hospital corridors were empty. It was dinnertime, an hour people from the Adirondacks were religious about. We took the elevator to the fourth floor and crept along the shiny linoleum, our sneakers squeaking, to room 403. I peered through the wired glass panel alongside the door, but my father was not there. There was just the single bed, still and white.

I pushed open the door. "In here," I said.

Sammy was lying on his side, away from us. His hair was longer, sliding over his face, and the skin of his cheek and arm were coppery with fading summer tan, healthy-looking against the white sheet. A few IV lines snaked along his tiny body. He looked peaceful. My stuffed animals ranged along the bedside table, but the yellow mane of a palm-sized lion peeked from under Sammy's arm.

Chad was still standing in the doorway.

"You can come in," I said. I went over and took his arm. "Did you bring the music?"

He held out the iPod. I put the ear buds in my ears and worked the volume, then went to the bed and held one bud to the ear just exposed from under the curl of sheet. Sammy murmured slightly and turned toward it, then he was still. I tucked the iPod under his pillow.

The hospital room was always cold. This evening it was glacial. Chad moved around, touching the telephone, the pole with its IV bags, circling like a plane trying to land, and I glared at the thermostat and fiddled until the air conditioning whirred off. In the silence we could hear Sammy's little snores, the hum of his breathing, which comforted me a bit. The gray blanket on the chair where my father usually sat was neatly folded. I shook it out and draped it around my shoulders. As if I had signaled him from some tower, Chad finally moved toward Sammy's bed.

About a foot from the metal side rail, he stopped.

"All those from you?"

"From the store down the street," I said. But I knew Chad wasn't really looking at the stuffed animals nor at me. He was staring at my brother.

I sat down in my father's chair, watching. What was Chad doing? Waiting for something to happen? Didn't he know better? I waited at least five minutes before he reached out and touched Sammy's ear. He adjusted the ear bud, lingering to stroke the edge of the ear, Sammy's light wisp of hair, his cheek. I knew how soft that cheek was. But I watched Chad as if he were my translator, the one speaking to my brother in ways I couldn't, his hands gentle and accurate.

He tried to cover Sammy's exposed arm, but the lion was in the way, so he set it with the other animals. "Don't," I said. He nodded and put it back but the movement had disturbed something in me. I pushed the edges of the gray blanket into my mouth, took it in my teeth, and bit down hard. Held myself there. Held my breath, until the threat of tears receded.

Chad found a straight back wooden chair and dragged it to the bed, pulling it so close he had to spread his knees wide to sit in it.

"I need to talk with him," he said, not looking at me.

"I thought I'd sit with him first." The book I'd brought to read to Sammy, once we were alone, felt heavy in my backpack, suddenly unwanted.

"Just five minutes." Chad's voice was apologetic but firm, like my father's when he made an unshakable decision. The edges of his face were soft, like he was going to cry too.

"Okay, five minutes." I got up wearily, gathering myself even tighter into the blanket. "Guess I'll wait outside."

The door closed behind me with an eerily silent whoosh. There was a padded black bench outside the door. I perched on the edge where I could watch Chad through the glass panel.

A rock of unfairness was settling in my chest, getting harder as I watched my neighbor scoot impossibly close to my little brother's bed, watched his head bend close to Sammy's ear, watched his shoulders jerk. So what if he was crying. I needed to cry too. He didn't seem to care that I was out in the hall, that I was watching him, bent and sloppy, pouring tears onto my brother's bed sheet. It felt like, despite so many vigils, despite the hospital becoming our most constant reality, I hadn't had more than two seconds alone with Sammy since the accident. Tonight it had looked possible. How come Chad Anderson got the odd grace this particular evening? Yes, we were lucky that my mother was late or had decided to stay home and sleep, that my father was gone. But why wasn't this luck my own?

The familiar loneliness rose up, carving its great hollow space. Since Sammy's disappearance from my every day, I couldn't hear him like I used to. I could hardly recall the way we stood together, making faces in the bathroom mirror, how he imitated me, how sure I was that he loved me. It was only my face reflected back to me now. The suspension of his life was a rattle, not a hum, in my head.

I thought of telling Zoe what it felt like. She wanted to be friends. Would she understand that he lived in a world I couldn't get to, what it was like not even to know if he'd come back? I wanted to tell her my dreams about the accident, unwinding each in my mind, and spreading them out for absolution. But I felt silenced by my own embarrassment of what was happening between us.

An idea had been forming with the passing days: Sammy not only held my past, he also had captured my future. As long as he slept, I had to be awake—with everything that had happened. As long as he was asleep, almost waking but not, I couldn't forget him, not for a millisecond. I couldn't leave this endless waiting because it could all change in the intake of one breath. He could die if I looked away. My mother had said, "We depend on life as we know it," and at the time, I thought that was silly. But it was true now. I wanted my life to be the same as it was before June fifteenth. Or, if not exactly the same—and here I thought of Zoe's gray eyes—at least predictably unexpected. Not this limbo of never knowing.

A digital clock by Sammy's bed marked our separation. It slipped into the next minute, and I stared at it. But Chad bent farther over the bed, whispering and taking his time, holding on to the railing like he was rooted. I couldn't imagine going in there while he was crying, no matter how mad I was. Nurses passing me down the corridor gave me little smiles of sadness, as if they knew I was the exile. I wanted to tell my brother that time had blurred memory. I wanted to ask, What color T-shirt did you wear in the boat that morning? Did you have your Yankees hat on? What color was the sky?

Although Chad's back was to the door, I could tell he was talking. Every now and then his hand would sweep the air in punctuation, like he was explaining a difficult math problem to my brother. He even stood up and shrugged off his Windbreaker, and I started to get up. But he settled and began again.

Eventually Chad wore himself out. I heard the door click. He held it wide, and I walked in. Everything was the same.

"I think he liked the music," Chad said.

We stood for a moment, watching the sheet rise and fall as my brother breathed. "I want a few minutes now," I said. I could feel pressure stinging behind my eyes, and I didn't want to cry in front of Chad. I walked toward the bed, grabbed the lion, and began to stuff it under the sheet, near Sammy's cheek, began to pull up the chair.

The door whooshed again.

"Molly?" My mother pushed into the room. She looked around quickly, as if she expected my brother to be gone.

"Chad Anderson drove me over," I said, willing any flush out of my face at the sight of her pale skin and dark-circled eyes. "We wanted to see Sammy."

She looked from one to another of us, not understanding. I could see she was really tired. "I can always bring you, Molly. Whenever you want to see him."

Yeah, but never alone, I wanted to tell her. I wanted to read to him, to make sure the music in the iPod wasn't too loud. If she'd only been five minutes later, I would've had time alone with him. I looked over at Sammy, debating whether to ask for those five minutes. I saw a strange look on my mother's face, hesitant, hoping, eager to be alone with Sammy herself. I wondered what she said to him, if she sang or listened or read aloud. I smoothed the sheet, covering the lion. My small gift, what I was allowed. It didn't take much space. *Just go home,* I told myself. "We've got to get back," I said. I picked up my backpack with the unread book and walked toward the door. Outside the hospital window, the light was changing toward evening. "See you in the morning," I told my mother. "Sleep well."

"I never sleep here." Behind me my mother set one of her carryalls on the chair Chad had vacated. The bag fell heavily, and I imagined stacks of mysteries, enough for ten days of reading.

Chapter 20

Midsummer Adirondack light stays long into evening. The western sky still glowed when we left the hospital. Chad didn't speak on the ride back to Cloud Lake, and even his driving was contained, as if he were operating his body via remote.

At the end of our driveway, I unstuck my sweaty legs from the vinyl seat and got out. Chad turned carefully, avoiding throwing gravel onto the finish of his brother's car.

When he was facing his parents' house, he leaned out the window. "Thanks," he said.

The drive had given me time. I felt calmed by the soft light. I grabbed my backpack from the well behind the passenger seat. "It's Okay," I said, lifting the backpack to one shoulder and starting down the path. "I'll probably see you around." Then I stopped, turned back.

"You're Okay, right?"

Chad's face was pale, the suntan almost gray, like all color had leached out in the past hour. He rubbed his palm along the steering wheel, making a slight squeaking noise, like a far-away bird.

"Did it help to see him?"

He stared at the trees. "It helped a lot."

"You get your iPod?"

"No. I left it with Sammy." Chad's hands quieted on the steering wheel. Now he was focused on me, eyes intent.

"What?" I said.

"Come here," he said.

I came back toward the car.

"I want to tell you something."

"What?" I said again, suddenly uneasy. Above us, birds were starting their evening songs, calling each other from the high branches of the cedars.

"You're so beautiful," Chad whispered.

"I'm what?" This didn't make sense.

Chad reached for my arm, pulled me slowly toward the car until the metal edge of the door was warm against my stomach. He tugged me closer, just as carefully as he had tugged Sam out of the tangled piles of weeds and rocks, until I was leaning toward his face.

It was a longer kiss this time. There was familiarity in the pressure of his lips now, but my stomach lay flat and unyielding.

I stepped back, waited. Late sun soothed my back, pines shushed the air. The roof of Chad's brother's car glittered like cherry candy.

"I don't get it," I said.

Chad was grinning. "You don't get it?"

"No."

"You don't get how I feel about you?"

"No." I took a breath as big as the sky. Inside, the anger of the afternoon waved over me, and its stoniness was good. "No," I said, my words coming out carefully, like each one cost a million dollars, "because we just visited my brother in the hospital and he may die and I don't even get to be alone with him for five minutes. Although you did, Chad. For fifteen fucking minutes you talked with Sammy. And then we had to leave. And you expect me to know what all of this means." I waved my arm toward the birds, the cedars, the smooth lines of his brother's car. "I didn't even get any dinner."

I was shrieking by that point. I didn't care. Chad's mouth was open, and I didn't care about that either.

"See you around," I said. I started down to the cabin, not letting myself listen to the car turning, to my so-called friend leaving me as quickly as possible.

By the time I got onto the front steps, my shirt was soaked with tears. I was glad my mother was at the hospital, and my father never noticed these things.

I didn't know Zoe's exact phone number. But I knew she was staying with her father in Lester's rental cabin. Zoe told me her father was a maniac about fishing, and the Ausable River was thick with trout. Phil Novato was a half-assed Hollywood agent, she said, who only worked with B-grade actresses. He liked roughing it on his vacations too. Zoe was grateful he left her at Cloud Lake every morning, grateful he spent most evenings with people he knew in Ausable Forks.

I paged through our booklet-sized phone book, looking for the party line extension for Lester's. She answered on the first ring.

"It's Molly Fisher," I said.

"Molly Fisher," she said. "What's cooking?"

"I wondered if I could come by," I said. "I could walk over. We could do something."

Zoe laughed, but it was friendly. "Like what?"

My palm was sweating. I transferred the telephone to the other hand. "Cards, I don't know. Anything."

"That sounds better than what I was doing."

I wanted to ask, What were you doing? But instead I just said, "I'll be over in fifteen minutes."

"You got any ice cream?" Zoe said.

"It might be kind of old."

"Bring it anyway. Just walk fast. We're in number five."

She hung up.

Although I stuck the half-carton of vanilla ice cream in a Ziploc bag and wrapped it in two dishtowels, by the time I reached cabin number five, my T-shirt had a large wet spot that smelled faintly.

"Vanilla," Zoe said, holding open the door.

"I better put it in the freezer."

She pointed. "Through there."

The cabin was tiny. Screened main room, a pinelog-paneled bathroom with fishing plaques, one bedroom. I saw walls of books, a chenille bedspread thick with roses, a red suitcase on the floor overflowing with clothes that looked like Zoe's.

"Nice place," I said.

"Not really."

I put the ice cream in the freezer. The entire kitchen was avocado green. There were three fishing rods by the back door, three creaky steps down to the lake. "Where does your father sleep?"

"He has a new girlfriend in town," Zoe said, coming into the kitchen. "Who is charmed by star stories. I never see him anymore."

"He just lets you stay here alone?"

"All the time," she said. She grinned at me, proving my memory about the gap in her front teeth. She walked over to the sink and ran the cold water, filled a glass. "Hey, I like your hair. Want some water?"

I fingered my braids and said no thanks. Everybody knew Lester pumped lake water, totally gross for anything but swimming.

Outside the lake itself was gleaming with almost sunset. I watched the water take on a shimmer of pink on top of the blue, like the inside of a shell.

Zoe came in, stood behind me and we watched the colors together. Then she said, "Have you been crying?"

I ducked my head. "What do you mean?"

"Your eyes are red. You look like you've been crying."

I moved closer to the kitchen window. "Are those fishing rods yours?"

"They're my father's. Why were you crying?"

"Because everything is screwed up," I said.

"I thought everything was going so well."

I was too tired to catch the layers of meaning Zoe always used. I shook my head. The view before me moved again as sun caught the silver sides of a motorboat going fast toward the Boat House. "Nothing's going well for me," I said.

Zoe plopped down in the ancient rocker and began rocking back and forth. She seemed to be waiting for me to tell her about my part in Sammy's accident, my stupidity. I ran my finger over the sill to catch a splinter, thinking about what I could say, and even more important why I felt I had to run over here today, why she was the first person I thought of when my world was falling apart. Could I tell her about Chad? Ask her why his kiss did nothing but make me mad? She thought boys were useless. Was I like her?

The silence grew around us, letting me think. In the blanket of peaceful waiting, the grip in my stomach began to ease. I took a deep breath.

"You heard about my brother."

Her rocker creaked rhythmically. "Sarah said something happened last month."

I was surprised to hear Sarah had held back. "His name is Sammy. He was in an accident on his birthday. He fell out of our motorboat and hit his head. Because of me."

She watched me closely. "Where is he now?"

"Plattsburgh."

"Is he Okay?"

I knew she meant, *Is he going to be Okay?*

"We don't know. The doctors don't know. He's been in a coma for twenty-eight," I corrected myself, "twenty-nine days."

The rocker protested as Zoe stood up. When she came over to me, I could feel her sudden warmth against my shoulder, and she leaned close like she had on the motorboat and at the Boat House that first evening, as if she wanted to fuse our skins. The hair on my arm knew it. It electrified toward her. But I didn't feel I wanted to move away this time, and after a few seconds, she gently put one arm around me then the other, holding me in a loop that felt amazingly like home.

I didn't mean to start crying again, but the tears came, silent at first. I buried my face in her shoulder, into the briny smell of Cloud Lake, the sunshine she absorbed as she skimmed along the water every morning. I soaked her heat into my body, chilled from the hospital room and the twenty-nine days that had passed so slowly and so quickly.

My father hadn't held me again after that one time in the car when we were coming home from the hospital. My mother felt so fragile, I was afraid it would be like hugging glass. Zoe's body was soft and welcoming, and it took me in like there was enough room for any pain I could surface.

At one point she reached for a tissue box, gave me a handful. I blew my nose and scrubbed at my eyes. Like my mother used to do when I was little, Zoe held out her hand and palmed the ball of tissues I gave her.

"You gonna keep them?" I said, like I remembered asking my mother. I was smiling a little.

"Probably will," Zoe said. She was looking at me, her eyes serious. "I think you've needed to do that for a while."

I nodded. "It's been awful."

"You could probably use talking about it," she said. "Have you talked about it?"

"Not really." I wanted to, so badly I didn't know where to begin. There was so much I missed about my brother. I wanted to tell her how I heard him singing, faint in the distance; I wanted to tell her about the time I was taking a shower and the hum of his voice was so loud, I turned off the water and stood there, naked and shivering. Listening with everything I had.

"You want to sit down?"

"No." I stared out at the lake again, at its constantly changing colors. A wind came up. The surface grayed then grew still deep blue.

"I took Sammy out for a motorboat ride," I began. "He was badgering me like you wouldn't believe. He said it was the only birthday present he wanted. He made a huge deal about it, even stole something from my dad. It was a mess." I thought about Sammy under the cabin, the light on the jackknife blade, how he sat the next evening on his big rock by the water, looking up at me, trying not to hope too much. "My father is real strict about the boat, so we had to go early in the morning. Before anyone was up."

I fingered a small red dish on the table by the window. It was painted with pink roses, chipped at the edge, and there was a dark burned spot as if someone had used it for an ashtray. The cabin smelled a little rank, but I hadn't noticed until now.

"Does your father smoke cigars?"

"It's totally disgusting," Zoe said. "It takes days to air out my clothes after he leaves."

I briefly thought of the red suitcase on the floor.

"What happened when you went out in the boat?" Zoe asked.

"We were doing fine until..." My breath caught, and I stopped.

"Until he fell," she said. She pulled the wad of tissues out of her pocket and handed them over. "Did he hit his head?"

"Yes." I blew my nose.

"You think it's your fault."

I nodded.

"Was it really?"

"Yes." But then I flashed on Sammy holding the knife. "No," I said. "It wasn't really. My brother had this birthday present, a jackknife from my father, and he dropped it in the lake. That was why it happened. It was partly my father's fault." I hadn't actually formed such a thought before, but saying it out loud made me feel incredibly light.

"Do your parents know?"

"No."

"But everyone would think now it was your fault. Your father, especially."

I nodded again, marveling at how clear it sounded when she said this, how amazing she knew this about my dad. Maybe Chad had talked. Maybe Sarah had said something about her uncle and what a total shit he was.

"I had a cousin who hit his head. He was in a coma for a year,"

Zoe said. "He's fine now." She was watching me. "People come out of comas, you know."

"It's just that..." I shrugged, helpless before her. "It's so confusing."

"Yeah," she said. "Life, huh."

I pressed the tissues to my cheek, my mouth, sucking at wetness. Zoe reached over and gently took them from me.

"We have a whole box," she said.

I smiled weakly.

"Did he give you hell?"

"My dad?" I shook my head. "That's what makes it worse. My mother won't listen to me, and my dad got really mad one time when I suggested going out in the boat to paint."

"I think not talking would be the worst thing."

"I guess we're all doing the best we can under the circumstances." I was trying to be fair, to present my family in a better light to this girl I didn't really know. But Zoe was smart. She didn't believe me and I could see it in her eyes.

"Looks like the sun's going to set soon," I said, to change the subject.

Outside the birds were doing their evening songs. Zoe went over and held the screen door open for me and we walked down to the flimsy dock Lester had built for the cabins. We sat at the very end, our feet dangling in the water, watching the lake change color to sunset. I let the light present the possibility I'd been feeling for the past hour: here was someone I could trust. Whiteface Mountain rose in dark contrast to the lemon sky. Soon the sky faded and a slip of crescent moon hung over the Boat House, and we could see the first stars.

When I laid a hand on Zoe's arm, the skin was warm. "Thanks," I said into the near dark.

She didn't dislodge my hand, just lay her own lightly on top. "We're good friends, Molly. What did you expect."

Chapter 21

We sat until it got dark enough for the mosquitoes, then we went back inside. Zoe turned on lamps, and I went to the fridge. I still hadn't eaten dinner. All the crying made me even hungrier.

"Can we eat something?" I said. "I don't really want ice cream."

"Anything you see is up for grabs." She came into the kitchen. "But we might want to hit the Boat House instead."

"Not tonight." I pulled out a white take-out box. "Is this still good?"

"It's from Nicola's. Two days ago."

I opened the container and sniffed. Chicken, tomato sauce, pasta. "Nicola's is great. We went there for my birthday last year."

"When's your birthday?"

"End of August." A saucepan hung on a nail over the sink. I dumped the chicken mess into it. "Always happens right before we close up the cabin and go back to the farm."

"I'll still be here," Zoe said, "I think." My heart emptied for a moment. "Phil's making noises about how great Ausable is, all his friends are here, blah, blah. Infamous Phil."

"Didn't he want to stay in Placid, in one of those big hotels?"

"I told you, he's into roughing it."

The chicken spit under the flame and I put an ill-fitting lid on top. Seemed like all cabins had ill-fitting lids. "Anything for salad?"

Zoe laughed. "You are a real gourmet."

"Not really. My mother is. She went to cooking school in Paris."

"No shit."

"Yeah. She's a really good cook. Much better than me." There was actually a head of romaine in the fridge. It looked Okay when I pulled off the top leaves. "Do you eat salad?"

"I eat anything." Zoe leaned back in the rocker. "I have to say that I can't quite figure you out, Molly Fisher." She said my name like she was tasting it.

I flushed, bent over the sink, began washing the lettuce. "Why is Phil infamous?"

"Surely you've heard of him. Phil Novato, agent to the Hollywood stars."

"Nope."

"That's good. He's a jerk. So are his movies." Zoe got up to find plates, silverware and folded paper napkins. She disappeared into the bedroom and came out with a Mason jar filled with slightly limp daisies. "Nice?" she asked, holding them up.

"Nice," I said, ladling chicken and pasta on our plates. I brought the salad to the table, and Zoe pulled the rocker closer.

She grinned at me, her mouth full. "I could get used to having you around."

It was dark when we finished eating. Zoe did a haphazard job with the dishes, stacking them in the drainer not even completely rinsed off. If my mother or Sammy did that, I usually came back into the kitchen after they were gone and rinsed everything again. But Zoe doing it didn't bother me. I just watched the way her arms danced from sink to drainer, and the clatter of cheap china and silverware soothed me in a way I hadn't felt in weeks.

She dried her hands on a dishtowel, left it wadded on the

counter, and pressed a button on the CD player. Light jazzy music filled the kitchen. A deep sax, piano, a sweet high voice scatting.

"What's this?"

"Macy Gray. I found it the other day in Saranac," Zoe said. She stood up, closed her eyes, and began to move. "I like dancing to it."

Jazz isn't exactly typical dance music. But Zoe didn't seem to know that. She just let her hips circle, her red hair sway across her cheekbones. In the harsh light from the fluorescents, her skin looked paler, more beautiful.

"Come on," she said. "I'm not looking."

"I don't dance."

"I've seen you dance." She moved toward me, her eyes slitted, and grabbed my hand, pulling me upright. "You just move to the sound, to how it feels in here." She pressed her free hand to her belly, listening. The hand moved to my stomach, and I almost jumped from the sudden heat. "In here," she said. "Where you feel things."

I didn't know thrilled and terrified could occupy the same space in my stomach but there they were. I was suddenly scared of everything she was showing me. Held like this, I couldn't move independently of her, and she seemed to know that, because she didn't let go of either contact, just began to sway again and all I could do was sway with her. At first I just followed, a clumsy mirror image of her, trying not to bump into table or chairs or counter. But after a few minutes the music seeped into me, like it had in the car listening to Chad's CD. I found fluidity in my legs, in my shoulders, in the heat of my neck and how my head felt resting there. The woman's voice climbed a ladder of notes, and my fingers climbed it too. I lifted my left foot, felt everything.

Zoe's eyes were still closed. She seemed to pause then imitate my movements, as I became the leader in our silky dance.

We never let go of each other. Our palms sweated and glued together. The feel of her hand on my belly translated down my legs. I found myself holding her shoulder, then the thin blade of it where it reached down her back. The song went on forever and I was grateful. When it stopped, we stayed still as the CD player clicked off, and Zoe pulled me toward her. It was a much different embrace than by the window. She just held me, and I was still in her arms.

When she let me go, we stood separate, not looking at each other. Evening air from the lake wafted over my skin, much too cool.

Chapter 22

When I got up the next morning, two new sketches of Sammy sat on the mantel. And my father was painting in the clearing. I made myself breakfast and went out to watch him.

He looked up from his easel and lifted a hand. "Come see."

The invitation was so totally unlike him, I almost choked on my toast. He even smiled at me as I walked down the path.

"Look at the light on those pears," he said. "How still it is."

I looked and saw movement. Flickers of sun and shadow, the trees leaning and dancing over us. But it was as if my dad's outdoor still life had inhaled and held its breath. The one I'd set up, that I loved for its uneasiness, was changed. The fruit now lay in a shallow basket woven in crimson and gold. Morning sun backlit the three Bosc pears, brown and long-necked, their cast shadows falling into deep purple on the red basket. My father had already layered the colors with an expert, quick hand so red shimmered through just enough that the shadows glowed even more than the light.

The pears' stillness and simplicity was totally different from anything he'd painted for many months. It was a statement of everything good and steady and predictable—qualities absent in our family this past year. As I studied the still life, I saw for the first time how my father held light captive. He sought the moment where nothing changed.

"What do you think?" He squinted at the painting, ready to criticize his work, a pastel stick held delicately between two fingertips like a forgotten cigarette. We were suddenly colleagues.

I didn't know what to say. "I like the shadows. Aren't you supposed to be gone to the hospital by now?"

"Your brother woke up last night."

Woke up? "Sammy's awake?"

"He's asleep now." My dad layered in a stripe of turquoise.

I tried to breathe deeply, stay calm. I couldn't. "We've got to go in," I said. "Right now."

"Your mother'll call us when he wakes up again."

"Are you sure he will?" I raised my voice. "Did the doctor say he would?"

"The doctor said there's a much better chance he will stay awake for good, now that he has started waking up." My dad finally put down the pastel stick and wiped his fingers on a rag. "I thought you'd be happy."

"I am happy," I said. Sensations pushed against my ribs, hurting and exhilarating. My hands were shaking. I jammed them in my pockets. "Can I come to the hospital with you?"

My father was closing the pastel trays and unpinning his paper from the easel board. "The doctor says it's better not to have too many people around during this stage. If..." he corrected himself, "when he wakes up again, we'll certainly bring you in to see him."

"You said I could go in whenever I wanted." I kicked at a pile of pine needles, my sneaker scattering them high into the air, landing close to my dad's painting. "It really sucks to break your promise." Inching my anger toward him, I watched his face for the rage I'd witnessed when he was splitting wood, telling me I'd gone too far. His hands hovered, paused, but they just tightened on the edge of his pastel box. He slowly snapped the case closed, the sound echoing sharp around us, saying everything.

"I know it doesn't make sense to you."

I didn't care anymore. "It's totally screwed. You know that."

"When the doctor says it's time, I'll drive you myself."

"That's not good enough," I said. "You know that too."

I'd never spoken to my father like this. It felt strange but strong.

The phone began ringing, the stutter that signaled our number on the party line.

"Your mother," he said. "The hospital." He wiped his hands hurriedly and ran toward the cabin. "Would you like the painting?" he said over his shoulder, taking the steps two at a time. "An early birthday present?"

"My birthday isn't for weeks!" I shouted, my eyes filling.

"Can you put those away?" he shouted back. "I may have to go into town."

But my mom just needed a friend's phone number. Sammy hadn't woken up again. I thought about spilling my father's pastel box all over the ground, saying it was an accident. But I carried it up to the porch, set it by the front door. I washed his colors from my fingers and wiped them dry on the dishtowel.

The painting I studied a long time, feeling its alien goodness. Finally I carried it down to the dock, the chalky side away from my body.

Chad's dock was two boat lengths from ours. He was sitting there, reading. I almost went back up to the cabin when I saw him but I didn't want to have to talk with my father or watch him get ready. Chad waved and disappeared into the thicket of shoreline birch, and a minute later he was next to me. I watched him sit down, his sunglasses hiding his face. I couldn't tell if he was still my friend. If he knew about my growing friendship with

Zoe. I just laid the painting on the dock, and we both studied it.

"My dad just did this," I said.

"He's a really good artist," Chad said, his voice neutral. "I bet his paintings sell for a lot of money."

"Yeah."

"So I'd better stay your friend because you'll be rich someday."

I knew he was kidding, trying to be friendly, trying to tell me we were Okay even though I didn't want to kiss him. In the bright sunlight, the painting's crimson and purple shadows shone even more intensely. I got up and set the painting on a flat rock in the shade.

"Actually, I'm not. He's only given me a little sketch each birthday. So don't hang out with me for the money."

Chad grinned then stretched back on the dock, his arms behind his head. When he closed his eyes, the lids were almost transparent, lined with thin blue veins. I tried to remember how Sammy's eyelids looked, but I couldn't even remember the color of his eyes for a moment. *Blue*, I told myself firmly. *Blue*.

"There's something else," I said. "Some good news."

Chad was silent. I thought he'd fallen asleep.

"Sammy," I said, my throat suddenly filled, "woke up."

The grin began again, spreading across Chad's face. "Excellent."

"He's not awake now," I said hurriedly. I traced lines on the dock with one finger, breaking up tiny pools of lake that reflected the intense sky. "And they don't know if he'll wake up again."

Chad, the Cloud Lake coma authority, dismissed my fear with one hand. "No, he will. That Web site said waking and sleeping was normal brain behavior. It's a good sign of complete recovery."

"You read about it on a Web site?" I hated him being right so much but I liked how *complete recovery* felt in my chest. "I want to go see him today."

"I'll take you." Chad's eyes were slitted, watching me.

"My parents want me to wait."

"I wouldn't wait."

The group of backlit Mergansers floated out from the rocks, making little duck noises. I thought of the moon coming out over the lake last night, the heat from Zoe's skin.

"I'd be happy to do it," Chad said. "I'd like to see him again too." He sat up, blinking, and stretched wide. I watched his arm muscles move under his T-shirt, imagined them gripping the motorboat's wheel. His face was already shiny with sweat.

"Aren't you driving for Zoe?" Even her name was hard to say out loud.

"Just this afternoon. Phil's in town. He may want to drive for her, if he isn't too wasted." I knew he was studying me, trying to figure me out.

"Let me know," he said.

"Okay," I said. "My parents are both home tonight." It was a first. "And I bet they go to bed early."

"How about eleven or so?" Chad unfolded himself from the dock and stood so tall above me that when I looked up, his face was in shadow. Light from the water glinted off his eyes. He began to pick his way off the dock, delicate as a cat, avoiding my dad's painting on its rock.

Chapter 23

When I walked back to the cabin, Sarah was there. She'd put her hair up, and it wisped across her cheeks and caught in the silver hoops that hung to her shoulders. She was in the swing, pumping herself back and forth like she was about to explode.

Aunt Anna was sitting nearby, her fists in the pockets of her baggy pink overalls, looking forlorn.

"We came to visit and nobody was here," she said.

"Mom's at the hospital," I said. "Dad's in the studio." I set down the painting, careful not to smudge the colors. "Do you want iced tea? It's instant."

"Iced tea sounds cooling." Anna mopped her upper lip. She reached for Sarah's magazine and fanned her face. "Your mother told us the good news about Sammy."

"You're getting the pages wet with your sweaty fingers," Sarah said.

"It's not really good news," I said. I moved toward the screen door, letting it slap my hip as I went into the kitchen. I stayed in front of the open freezer for a while then poured the iced tea, adding a glass for my cousin.

"I don't drink instant," she said when I brought it outside.

"Nobody's forcing you."

Anna sipped cautiously, studying me over the rim of her glass. "It is good news about Sam, don't you think? There's a good chance he'll wake up again."

That was Chad's line too. Anna's eyes were narrowed, trying to convince herself, all of us. Condensation was running wet strips down her glass and she pressed the coolness to her face. "Do you have lemons?"

"We don't do lemons these days," I said, but she had already gotten up, the screen door slapping behind her as she moved toward the kitchen. Thunder rippled in the distance, breaking the still afternoon. Sarah pumped the swing and read her magazine.

"How's Mark?" I said finally.

Sarah's tone was dangerous. "He's fallen for that butch in the band."

"Lisa?"

"Who else?"

Sarah flipped pages so fast they crackled.

"That sucks," I said.

"They're both fucked up. They deserve each other." She bent her head, reading. "Maybe I should take this quiz. *How to Tell If Your Man's a Loser—Before He Breaks Your Heart.*"

She got up, whacking the magazine onto the swing seat. "I'm going to visit Chad Anderson. He lives around here, doesn't he?"

"He's driving for Zoe."

"So I'll wave from the dock." Sarah was grappling with the rustic railing as she worked the stairs in her stupid sandals. "That girl is one different chick," she said, turning to stare at me. "Better watch out for her."

Anna came back outside as I was trying to think of an intelligent answer. I must have blushed.

"Zoe?" I said.

Anna sat heavily, pushing up her bangs. "Who's Zoe?"

"Not like us." Sarah sent this important message to the trees and disappeared down the path.

Anna leaned back, gathering wild curls with both hands and a rubber band. She was looking at me, puzzling.

"What?" I said.

"Nothing." My aunt fanned her face. "What did they tell you, exactly? About Sammy?"

"Not much." My voice was suddenly as sullen as Sarah's.

"Did they tell you about the tests?"

"No."

"Or that Sam's prognosis is quite good now that he's woken up once?"

How did anyone know for sure? An image came of Sammy under the cabin, the light slanting through the dirt haze, haloing his hair to gold. "What's a talisman?" he'd asked me, when I said the jackknife was Dad's talisman and that's why he had to give it back. "It's magic, something that makes us feel loved. Like you do," I'd said, "for me."

My aunt saw my face. "Sammy wanted that lion first thing when he woke up," she said.

Her kindness made me smile. I picked up a lemon slice and began squeezing it a little, inhaling the sharp citrus burst.

A boat engine revved near our dock then rumbled to an idle. Then voices, Sarah's, another's that wasn't Sarah's that caused me to sit taller in my chair. In a few minutes, Zoe's red head shot up like a flare on the path. She'd been running but looked fresh out of the water.

"Molly Tamale!" she called, her smile huge.

Everything swam for a moment, then righted itself. I stayed glued to my seat. If I got up, there would certainly be a long sweaty mark from my legs.

"That's Zoe," I told my aunt, as we watched Zoe run up. "She's renting down at Lester's."

"Hi," Zoe said, breathless.

"Hi," I said, breathless too.

There was a pause.

Anna broke the silence. "How do you stand it at Lester's?"

Zoe's face relaxed. She grinned at Anna. "I can put up with a lot if I can waterski every day."

"Oh, the water-skier," Anna said. "I watched you the other morning. You're sensational."

"This is my aunt, Anna Fisher. Zoe's won all these awards." Catching myself babbling on, I cleared my throat, finished with, "She's even skiing at Daggett Lake in August."

"That's cool. Want some tea?" Anna asked.

"It's instant," I said quickly, but Zoe said, "Sure."

Zoe sank down on the swing Sarah had vacated. She poked at the little dish of sliced lemons. "Fancy."

"Anna."

"I like her."

"She's the only normal person in this family," I said.

"What about you?" Zoe said.

I stared at the bird feeder. The air was so hot, I'd burn myself if I touched my own cheek. "Pretty far from normal, I guess."

"That's good news." Zoe pushed with her feet and the swing swept back. A high laugh rang up from the dock. "Sarah's mooning over Chad. I think she likes him."

"We should warn him."

"He can take care of himself." Her eyes were nailing me to my chair. "Do any dancing today?"

"Nobody to dance with." I picked up Sarah's magazine and fanned myself.

Anna was coming through the screen door with another sweating glass. She handed it to Zoe who gulped half of it.

"Easy to fix that," Zoe said, setting the glass down with a little gasp of satisfaction.

"Fix what?" Anna said. The bib of her overalls ballooned away from her chest as she sat again.

"Zoe's water ski," I improvised. "She even skis on plywood."

"No kidding."

"On a huge circle of it," I said. "It was invented in Hawaii. They are really expert water-skiers there. It turns as she's skiing."

"Most of the time I don't fall off." Zoe was grinning at me, her new PR agent, and her foot began jiggling like it was aching to slip into a ski binding.

From the waterfront we could hear Sarah's laugh again. "Want to go rescue Chad?" I picked up my glass and Zoe's, pushed myself out of my chair.

"Leave those," Anna said. "I have to wait for Sarah. Might as well relax for a while."

"I'm a big fan of relaxation myself. Like dancing." Zoe was still sitting. She scanned the magazine I'd set down again on the swing seat, opened to the page with the quiz. "Or this intelligent magazine. *How to Tell If Your Man's a Loser—Before He Breaks Your Heart.* You gonna take that quiz, Molly?"

As usual, I heard the layers of meaning in her question. Was I like her, *one different chick?* She waited, eyes dark gray in the shadows of the porch.

My pulse jitterbugged for a second. "I don't need to take that quiz."

She put the magazine down. "Me neither."

Anna was really scanning our faces now. I looked back at her, as innocent as possible, my expression saying, *There's nothing going on, nothing to figure out.* Hiding the imprint on my skin from the dancing, afraid it was surely visible from the heat it radiated even after twelve hours. At that thought, I crossed my arms, hoping Zoe wasn't seeing anything either.

"Sarah is the only one with a boyfriend," I said, to distract all of us. "Or twenty."

Sarah's voice trickled up the hill again. "Twenty-one, if she's having any luck with Chad Anderson," her mother said.

Zoe got up. "Thanks for the iced tea, Mrs. Fisher."

"Anna. Maybe I'll get to see you ski on that plywood thing sometime."

"It's awesome," I said.

"Molly's my biggest fan." Zoe linked her arm under my elbow and pulled me toward the steps. We stumbled down them, joined, giggling a little, then Zoe let me go. She galloped ahead of me down the path, her Indian Paintbrush hair bouncing in the sunlight.

Chapter 24

When we arrived at the dock, Sarah was sitting on one of the boat benches, using her hands to tell some story. Chad bent over the outboard motor. He was pulling long weeds from the propeller.

"Almost got this fixed," Chad said, interrupting Sarah. "You want to ski the north end of the lake?"

"Crossovers," Zoe said. "I need a partner."

I shrank back, but Zoe was watching Sarah.

"You ski?"

My cousin looked quickly at Chad. I could see her tiny brain calculating the effect of a bathing suit and the risk of lying. Even though she lived in Florida half the year, she hated getting wet. "Some," she said.

"You have your suit with you?"

Sarah slowly lifted her tank top. An apple-green string bikini top was underneath. She kicked off her skinny sandals and unzipped her shorts, slid them down her legs to reveal the bikini bottoms, barely a scrap of cloth in the same color. Chad was watching closely. Then I noticed Zoe was too, her eyes narrowed.

There was silence.

Finally Zoe nodded. "Nice suit." She became businesslike. "*Chad* and I wondered if you could help us for an hour or so. I need to practice these slalom crossovers, and Molly here has finked out on us." She winked at me, taking the sting out of her words.

"Because of the accident," Sarah said, as tactlessly as possible. She was folding her shorts and top, piling them on the seat. "Molly won't even get in a motorboat."

"Actually," Zoe said, "she has gotten in this very motorboat. But unfortunately she doesn't ski. Which is why Chad suggested you."

Chad looked at Zoe, surprised.

"Didn't you, Chad?" Zoe prompted.

"Sure," Chad muttered. He bent back over the propeller. "Be great if you could help us out."

Zoe pulled off her own tank top. I thought she could tell I was watching her now. Her deeply tanned shoulders were flushed with pink sunburn and freckles. "How about we start with a few circles at the north end of the lake." She pointed Sarah toward the pair of regular skis near the bow of the boat. When my cousin's smile began to falter, Zoe added, "You'll look great on water skis. Don't you think so, Chad?"

Chad straightened up, the look on his face a mix of resignation and lingering interest in Sarah's string bikini. "Thanks for helping us out," he said again.

Sarah nodded graciously. She looked at me, assessing the competition.

"I'm going to stay here, catch up on my reading," I said, wondering why, once again, I was so determined to paint myself out of any picture.

It was at least an hour before I heard the boat engine growl as it downshifted near our dock. Zoe's voice, indistinct, called goodbyes, then the boat pulsed away.

Sarah appeared on the path, carrying her spiky sandals. Her

wet hair traced rivulets along her bare shoulders. The wet bikini outlined under her tank top now didn't look sexy at all. In fact, the top was streaked with mud. She didn't seem to notice.

Anna looked up from her book. "How did it go?"

"Only fell twice." My cousin sat in the wicker chair, water pooling on the floor near her feet. "I was totally awesome."

"You both used to love the water," Anna said. "You skied on this lake when you were kids."

"Except Sarah hates getting wet," I said.

"Well, I love it now."

I had the sudden image of Zoe's interested eyes, looking at Sarah's tiny bikini.

Sarah pulled my drying towel from the railing, squeezed it around her hair. "Zoe says waterskiing's like riding a bicycle. She says you don't forget."

"I bet you wiped out on the crossovers," I said.

"Splattered myself all over the lake. I totally forgot to let go of the towrope." She pressed the edge of the towel into her ears. Without the gobs of makeup she usually wore, her skin glowed. "Zoe showed me how to keep my balance. She says you just pretend you can stand on the water and let the boat carry you."

"She can ski on plywood," Anna said.

"She's awesome," Sarah said. "She showed me this cool trick when we did crossovers."

"How's Chad?" I asked.

Sarah shrugged. "He doesn't talk much." She shook her hair free, began finger combing it. "When we did crossovers . . . "

I got up. "I'm starved. Does anyone want a sandwich?"

"I want to finish my sentence, Molly Fisher." Sarah glared at me. "Anyone would think you were jealous that I got to go waterskiing and you sat up here like an old person, reading."

"Not everyone who reads is an old person," Anna said mildly. "And yes, I'm up for a sandwich."

"I'm not," Sarah said. "I'm meeting Chad and Zoe for hamburgers at the Boat House." She paused. "Molly, you want to come?"

"No," I said. "I've got plans." The last thing I wanted to do was sit with my cousin and Zoe, totally left out as they talked about awesome crossovers. Not about dancing. Or looking at stars.

"Okay." Sarah sounded relieved. "I'll bring the car back in an hour."

Anna looked at her watch. "If you do I'll miss the bank. I'll drop you." She stood up, and Sarah did too. I was the only one left sitting.

They gathered up their things. Sarah, whose personality had changed completely with her amazing skiing experience, even hung my towel back over the railing.

"I take back what I said about your friend Zoe," she whispered in my ear, giving me a little goodbye hug. "She's awesome."

My face flushed. I'd never felt so jealous in my life. *Yeah*, I thought. *You said that like fifty times.*

That evening, before I went to meet Chad for our secret hospital trip, my mother told me Sammy woke up again. This time he opened his eyes and said, "Mommy." Although he fell back asleep right away, my parents were giddy. The doctor still wanted as little stimulation as possible—"It's a delicate time," my mother said—so my parents, as much as they wanted to, didn't stay overnight. I tried again for a legitimate visit that evening, but my father was firm.

"We have to think of Sammy's welfare first," he said.

"I am!" I shouted and stomped out on the porch in the dark, away from both of them. I looked around for something to throw. What if he woke up in the middle of the night and didn't remember who I was? My bones ached at the idea. Then I thought of something worse. What if he woke up remembering me and how I'd shown off, how I'd turned the boat and made him fall? I had to get to the hospital before that happened, explain everything, tell Sammy again how sorry I was. I would cover for anything he ever did for the rest of his life, take the blame for every small theft.

The book my father had been reading hit the porch stairs with a satisfying smack.

Chad wasn't waiting at the road at eleven. Even with a flashlight, it was hard to follow the path to his parents' cabin. When I scratched on his screen, Chad just mumbled in his sleep.

I whispered, "It's Molly," as loud as I dared. But he snorted, flipped over, and began snoring.

"Chad," I whispered louder, "Chad?" I caught the whimper in my voice. I moved the cabin door handle silently a few times then went to stand in the heated dark outside his bedroom window.

His snores rattled the wood frame. I gave up.

I sat on the dock a long time, sobbing into my sweatshirt. Nobody in the world was my friend. And soon not even Sammy would be.

By two, when it started to rain, I walked up to my father's studio and sat on the floor, studying Sammy portraits by flashlight. The portraits were beautiful in the dim light.

My father had worked on them a lot, but they were still of a little boy sleeping, not a little boy awake.

I remembered last week, when my father was sitting on the porch reading the paper, I had carefully carried out a painting from the mantel.

"Can I ask you something?"

He rustled the pages, not looking at me. "Okay."

"About this," I said, forcing him to look up. Watching his face change as he saw the painting he'd done. My father had told me once a painting was finished, it became its own self, something so apart from him he hardly remembered making it. "I wanted to ask about this shadow."

I was pointing to a violet red streak under Sammy's closed eyes. I hadn't seen my father use red in shadows before.

His face softened even more. "That was a lucky moment," he said. He took a big breath, as if remembering the miracle of it.

"What made you see it?"

He thought for a long minute. "It was very late one night. I was watching his breathing."

"Yeah," I said. I knew how to do that.

"And I saw the red there. It was beautiful." My father had

shrugged, as if that were the explanation for everything.

I went back to the cabin, crept to my bedroom. Under my pillow was my small collection of talismans, the few things I'd gathered since the accident, to remind me who I was and help me believe Sammy still loved me and would come back.

I sat on the floor by my bed and spread them on the red and orange rug, studying them by the flicker of my almost-spent flashlight: Sammy's fire engine, the blue puzzle piece, the miniature stuffed bear in its red Santa Claus hat. I basked in their colors, bright and primary enough for hope.

In the next sleeping porch, my father was snoring. My mother was making little cries as she slept. I fell asleep there on the rug, clutching my good memories, my talismans, in a stupor from the insistence of the rain.

Chapter 25

Rain continued all the next morning, and my parents left for the hospital without me. Aunt Anna came over and after five minutes decided I was mopey and needed her help.

We would have an outing.

Anna's outings usually involved getting lost on Adirondack back roads, peeing in the bushes and eating stale Hershey bars from her glove compartment. But there wasn't really an alternative. Wait by the phone for Zoe to call? Read my book, convince myself that I wasn't really lonely?

I said yes. I agreed on an outing if we kept to towns.

Anna chose Willsboro. The ferry crossed Lake Champlain near Willsboro. Willsboro had lots of possibilities. Anna had researched it on the Internet.

She spun her station wagon out of the driveway and floored it. "Willsboro's chamber of commerce lists fifteen antique stores. Bounty practically next door."

I fiddled with my seat belt. "This is broken."

"Sarah jammed it the last time she borrowed the car."

It was so tight, I couldn't even fasten it comfortably. "Who'd she have in here?"

"Her friend Zoe."

Her friend? Sarah and Zoe had been riding around in my aunt's car, talking about waterskiing and how awesome everything was. It made me want to barf.

"Some concert in Saranac last night." Anna bounced past a pothole, gave me a sideways glance. "They didn't call you?"

They hadn't.

"I didn't want to go." I slid low in the seat, so if we passed a cop, my aunt wouldn't get in trouble.

Anna pushed on the accelerator and rain streaked across the windshield faster than the wipers could keep up.

"So, where are we starting?"

"This great place, Margaret Somebody's." Anna swerved to avoid a dead raccoon, and I was flung into the door.

"What are you hunting?"

My aunt's outings were hunts. She hunted outlandish items for no money. Not hard in our part of the world. The last purchase had been a flat-topped straw hat with fuzzy balls on strings. Anna swore it stymied black flies.

"Something red. Cheery. We all need cheery right now, especially you." She patted my knee.

I saw zero red in the towns sodden with rain on our way to Lake Champlain. The lake ran half the length of the eastern Adirondack Park, forty minutes from Cloud Lake if my aunt drove. Even at nine on a Wednesday, Willsboro was still sleepy, except for the coffee shop near the ferry docks. But my aunt turned onto a side street and there was the store, a neon Open sign flickering in the window.

"Margaret never closes." Anna got out, slammed the door. "Come on, Molly."

Margaret's dirt driveway was full of puddles. Anna, wearing her duck shoes, splashed toward the porch. Like so many Adirondack homes turned store, Margaret's entrance was piled with apple crates and tin milk cans and plaques about fishing and *Welcome to Our Cabin* signs. But inside, a ceiling fan fluttered the silk fringes of a hundred red lamps, creating the effect of a cheerful whorehouse.

My aunt stood in the doorway, her face pink with happiness. "Margaret?" she called, walking toward a back room. "It's Anna Fisher. I phoned yesterday."

I wandered, avoiding tiny end tables stacked with china dogs and wicker baskets. Shelves full of tattered paperbacks hugged one corner. An empty, sagging armchair was stacked with more books. I set them on the floor and sat down in a puff of dust.

I was halfway through *The Lion, the Witch, and the Wardrobe*, one of my favorites, when Anna returned, laden with red.

"Looks like you scored," I said.

"Big time. Look at this." She held out her arms.

Tablecloths. All covered with bright red splotches. "Cherries?" I guessed.

"Aren't they gorgeous." She dumped the tablecloths on the chair I'd just vacated. "Did you look around any?"

I put the book aside. "Something cool over here," I said.

She came over to where I was standing. We peered down at a glass case full of army stuff. Canteens, dog tags, even a moldy ration book. "Old stuff. French," I said, trying to read the writing.

"Look at that." Anna was pointing to a jackknife I hadn't noticed. "Exactly like your father's." She raised up. "Margaret," she hollered. "We need you."

A doughy woman in a print muumuu ambled out of the back room. "Whatcha find? That's the real stuff." She peered at me. "Your girl don't look so good."

"I'm Okay," I said, though the edge of the metal case was suddenly searing my palms.

"This knife." Anna pressed one finger against the glass top. "My brother's got one exactly like it."

"You want to see it?"

I nodded.

Margaret moved slowly to the case, slid open the back. "You could've gotten it out yourself. I don't lock anything." With a little clunk, she set the jackknife on the counter.

Anna picked it up, opened it carefully. "The blade is perfect."

"No rust," Margaret said. "It's not that old."

"Vietnam War," I said.

Her eyes narrowed at me. "Right you are."

I moved closer to Anna. "There's even a screwdriver," I said. I reached for the knife. Its weight felt good in my hand.

"I'm getting it. Add it to Anna's cherries."

Chapter 26

Down Margaret's driveway, two boys Sammy's age were riding past in the rain, the wheels of their red bicycles flickering, clacketing from the colored plastic strips in the spokes. I watched them careen around a corner, one of the boys standing up on his pedals, his bike swerving from the imbalance of weight.

I reached into my pocket and pulled out the knife. Flicked it open, held it up to the dull rain light. "These are really well made," I said. "Army issue."

"I find this family's fascination with knives truly weird," my aunt said. But she still didn't start the car.

"Dad's knife was a gift from Willie, his buddy who died in the war."

"Your father never let anyone touch that knife. Too much associated with it."

"Mom won't tell me anything else about it."

"She doesn't know." Anna was silent, as if making up her mind. "Melvin told me one night when I caught him crying."

I marveled at that. I'd never seen my father cry.

"It helped me understand him." She took a deep breath. "This isn't easy stuff."

"I can handle it."

"He and Willie were best buddies in the war. But then your father caught Willie with a young man from the village."

"Caught him? How?" But already my mind was imagining.

"They were holding each other, kissing. Men can love each other that way, just like men and women."

"I thought my dad would be cool with that stuff," I said carefully.

"Your dad was nowhere near cool. He was just a kid from a small Adirondack town. So he got into a big fight with Willie. The gift of the knife was Willie's apology. But he got killed before Melvin could reconcile his feelings."

Something didn't make sense. "If the knife is so precious to my father, why was he giving it to Sammy for his birthday?"

Anna snorted. "No way he was giving a knife to a six-year-old."

"A seven-year-old."

"Still." Anna sat, turning the idea in her mind. "I don't know. Maybe because the knife is some kind of legacy? Something precious because it holds memories?"

Anna was quite the psychotherapist. "How does Dad feel now about people loving each other that way?"

"I have no idea. We don't talk about that kind of thing." She watched me watch the driveway. "If your dad never let you touch Willie's knife, how did you know about the screwdriver?"

"Sam showed me."

"Now I'm totally lost."

Rain was coming down in earnest now, pounding the car. It felt like we were underwater, enclosed in a cocoon where we could still breathe. The pulse in my stomach began thrumming up to my throat, loosening it. I rolled up the window until only a hint of rain-scented breeze came up from Lake Champlain.

"Sammy stole Willie's knife. The day of the accident. Daddy promised to give it to him for his birthday, but Sammy wanted it sooner. He called it borrowing. He did it a lot."

"He stole things? A lot?"

"Yeah. Dad blamed me when something went missing. Mom knew it was Sammy, but Dad didn't believe her."

"Why didn't you tell him?"

"Dad doesn't believe me either." I shrugged. "And Sam was so little. He never meant to do anything wrong."

"But it is wrong, Molly."

I couldn't explain it, even to myself.

"Each time Sammy took the knife, I put it back for him. Dad forgets to lock the studio."

"How many times?"

"Three, four," I said. *Ten, fifteen.* I ran one finger down my side window. Talking had fogged us into our own little world. I inched the window down again, and the lake breeze came in strong.

"And you put it back that morning, before the accident."

I could feel her staring at me. "Not that morning. I actually didn't know Sammy had taken Willie's jackknife until we were out on the lake."

Anna was silent for a long time. I could almost hear her brain clicking, putting the pieces together. "My brother promises Sammy the jackknife, a deranged idea, and Sammy, being a kid, takes it. You put it back for him. Then he takes it again." She looked at me. "So you put it back Tuesday? After you came back from the hospital?"

The bright morning, the breeze ruffling my Windbreaker, the growl of the boat engine—it flooded back to me on this gray day in a sharp whistle of energy. I heard Sammy's voice saying, "I just saw a really big fish."

"He was just holding it. Then he began playing with it. He was in the stern, and I didn't see him because the sun was in my eyes. I think he must've dropped it. I guess it fell in the lake, and he started reaching for it, and . . . "

"Wow," Anna said. "Wow."

It was a satisfying response. The boys on their red bicycles raced by, puddles leaping over their shoes. I rolled up the window completely until the clear strip of world blurred back into rain-streaked glass. "Can we go home now?" I said.

My aunt put her hand on my leg and squeezed a little, then she glided the car back onto the shiny wet blacktop. "What does your father think happened to the knife?"

"Everyone's been so busy with the hospital and all." I shrugged. "Or maybe he thinks I lost it. Another reason to hate me." My hands were clenched so tightly between my legs, they ached. I flexed my fingers. "Can we turn on the heater?"

She flicked a knob and the car filled with dusty warmth. "Your father doesn't hate you, Molly. He loves you. He's just . . . the way he is. He was always very private, very intense, even before the war and Willie's death. If you love him, you adapt, appreciate the talent, the good moments." She shrugged. "Thank God most of us aren't that complicated."

I didn't answer.

"You could just put this one in his studio." She shook her head, as if it were a stupid idea, as if she didn't like lying either but she would consider it to avoid dealing with my dad. I understood this, but there was one basic flaw.

"He's an artist," I reminded her. "He'd see it wasn't the same knife."

"But wouldn't it be a cosmic joke on him, if he stayed so distracted he never looked?" Then she sighed. "We're kidding ourselves. He'd notice a hair out of place."

"I guess he's really distracted if he's forgotten the knife."

"That's just temporary," my aunt said. "Once Sammy's better, it'll all go back the way it was before the accident."

For some reason, this made me feel instantly sad. I stared out the smeary wet windows, hypnotized by the unending blur of gray and green. Thought of my mother's unhappiness, the inevitability of a final escape. The distance and hurt in my father's eyes when he looked at her and couldn't have her. The accident was holding my mother here, binding her to us, and it was requiring my father to care.

The hum of our tires on the wet road almost sounded like singing. We merged onto 9N near Ausable Chasm, passing the big sign and gift shop. There were already a few cars idling outside, even on this rainy morning.

"I always wanted to take Sammy to Ausable Chasm," I said.

"I've never been there."

"Me neither. All these years. You'd think there would've been a school trip or something."

"What will you do with the knife?" my aunt asked, not looking at me.

"Give it to Dad, I guess." But I didn't want to. I wanted to keep it for a while, although I wasn't sure why.

Chapter 27

When Anna let me out at the driveway, I went straight to the cabin. The new knife lay neat inside my jeans pocket, the heft of it, the fake wood handle, bumped my leg as I walked. Rain was clearing, the woods smelled wet and cedary.

In the kitchen, my mother was making soup. It smelled good. I leaned against the counter, watching her. Her hands were efficient, chopping onions.

"Anna bought tablecloths," I said. "Ugly red ones with huge cherries."

"Oh, Anna." She shook her head and kept rummaging in the cupboard above the stove, pulling out three spice jars.

"You and Dad used to buy antiques. There's still some under the cabin."

"When were you last under the cabin?"

I jammed my hands in my pockets, against the knife. "Did anyone call?"

"Your friend Zoe."

"Zoe Novato?"

"What other Zoe do you know?" My mother dumped the spices into the garbage and set the jars in the sink. "She sounded impatient to talk to you."

"She sounded impatient?"

My mother looked at her watch. "There's an echo in here. And I've got a run to make before dark. Can you watch this pot?"

I was sure Zoe was out on the lake with Sarah. But I dialed her number anyway. When she answered, I couldn't talk for a moment. I'd forgotten the low rumble of her voice and how it scratched at my skin.

"It's Molly," I finally said. "Fisher."

"I know your last name."

She did.

"My mother said you called. Early."

"Where were you, early?"

"Out," I said. "Where were you?"

"What do you mean?"

"I mean, where have you been?"

"I've been water skiing," Zoe said mildly.

My cheeks felt hot. This wasn't going like I'd hoped. "With Sarah, I bet."

"So?"

"The Cloud Lake crossover queens." I could hear the annoying whine in my voice, but I didn't stop. "Totally awesome."

"What's that supposed to mean?"

"Never mind," I said. "I shouldn't have called."

I slammed the phone down. It rang again immediately.

"What?" I said.

"Don't you hang up on me until you tell me why you haven't returned my calls."

"What calls? I only got one message. Today. And I called you right away." Steam rose from the soup pot. The lid jiggled. I lowered the flame even more.

"You are such an idiot. I called twice since I saw you with your aunt. Left two long messages with your father." I could hear the question in her voice.

"I never got any messages." My father had finally installed a phone line in the studio. Of course he'd be answering the phone. It could be the hospital calling.

"He promised to tell you."

I thought of the pad by the studio phone, full of my dad's neat handwriting. Messages he'd been too distracted to give me. I hadn't thought to read what that handwriting said.

"He didn't give you any message from me?"

"Not one." I felt suddenly, unexplainably giddy. Like I could twirl right there, in front of my mother's soup pot. Do a grand jeté across the kitchen. But I held back. There were still questions.

"You and Sarah have sure gotten friendly."

"I made a deal with Chad," Zoe said carefully. "He drives the boat, I keep Sarah busy."

"I thought you liked Sarah." *More than me.*

Zoe laughed. "And I thought you were mad at me."

"Mad at you? About what?"

"The dancing."

"The dancing," I said. "No, I wasn't mad about the dancing." It was hard to believe a person's body could hold it all: the relief of talking with her, the generous pity now I felt toward Sarah who had no clue, the giddiness of remembering the night we danced.

Zoe's voice was suddenly bright, even brisk. "So when do you want to get together?"

"I'm watching soup right now." I looked at the big kitchen clock. It was red and white, shaped like a teapot. One of my Aunt Anna's discoveries that my mother actually liked. "For another fifteen minutes. Anyway, aren't you practicing crossovers?"

"My feet are worn out. Something's wrong with the new bindings, they make my toes numb."

"And it's raining," I said.

"Yeah," said Zoe. "I'm getting tired of racing across the lake with my eyes closed. What time can you be over here?"

As I hung up, I thought of her gray eyes. I imagined them squinting against driving water above and below her as she skimmed the surface of Cloud Lake. I wondered what she saw through all that wetness, if her world was liquid too.

There was remembered tension in my body now, welcome and focused, like I used to feel at the barre. I noticed it putting on my socks, my newest pair of sneakers.

Chapter 28

Zoe wanted to climb.

She was already dressed for a hike, in a silvery long-sleeved top that made her look like Wonder Woman and threadbare socks.

"You need two pairs if you're going to wear those." I pointed to her feet. "Unless you want monster blisters."

"You and your rules." She yanked off the socks and went to get a better pair. "Next you'll want us to bring a lightning rod because it's raining."

Rain was thrumming the cabin roof but there was no thunder.

"Hikers don't carry lightning rods," I said, adjusting the toppling stack of newspapers on her kitchen table.

She sat with a thump. "Are you sure? I don't want to get struck by lightning. The contest at Daggett Lake is in four weeks."

"A person doesn't get struck by lightning," I said, "if there's no thunder." Mountaintops in the Adirondacks were mostly open summits, and nobody in their right mind hiked when there was threat of lightning. As I explained this, Zoe began grinning again and I felt my face flush as I realized she was teasing me. I stared at the stack of newspapers. "You read all these?"

"Just for the weather." Zoe finished pulling on the socks. "For your information, it's going to clear."

"I heard it on the car radio."

"I didn't think you drove."

"I was shopping this morning with my aunt. She bought these disgusting tablecloths." I watched Zoe force a pair of antique sneakers on her feet, without untying the laces. I couldn't resist saying, "Those are full of holes too."

She held up a sneaker-clad foot. "I've walked miles in these."

"No kidding."

"They're absolutely fine." She stood up. "And so am I, now that you're here." She gave me a quick hug. "I really missed you."

I felt the flush return.

"Do I need a jacket?" she asked. I shook my head, dumb. She grabbed one anyway. "So your aunt got tablecloths. What did you get?"

The words were out before I could grab them back. "A jackknife," I said.

Zoe stuffed the jacket in a daypack. Then she disappeared into the kitchen and came out with a little bag. That went into the pack too. From where I sat I could see the kitchen table, the CD player. I thought about her arms circling my back, dancing me across the tiny kitchen, and wondered if Zoe listened to Macy Gray when she was here alone. I didn't want to wonder if she danced with anyone else.

"It's just an ordinary jackknife," I added.

"Jackknifes aren't exactly ordinary in your family."

"My aunt found it, actually." As if that made a difference. "I just bought it."

"Have you told them what really happened?"

"Just Aunt Anna."

She was busy with the pack, not looking at me. "You know your parents will blame you forever. Even when Sammy gets better, everyone will still think you caused the accident unless you say something."

"Maybe I *did* cause the accident. It was my decision to take the boat out that morning. Nobody else had anything to do with it." I tasted the words, but I really no longer believed them.

"We both know better than that," Zoe said. "It was someone else's fault too. You just need to tell him, and things will be a lot better."

Like some kind of soppy Hollywood effect, at that moment the clouds broke suddenly, letting a square of sunshine into the room. It fell on the table between us and lit up the cracked red linoleum. I got to my feet.

"You want to climb or what?"

In the summer trees above the trail, cicadas that hadn't seen sun for weeks hummed like a choir. I gave myself over to moving my body in time with their rhythm, following Zoe who bounded ahead like we were in a race. I did my best to avoid the largest of the puddles on the trail, but like my Aunt Anna, Zoe went right for them. Soon her sneakers were black with mud, her calves speckled with dark dots.

She passed me her water bottle. "You haven't even told your mother?" she asked, continuing the conversation I had short-circuited at her house.

I took a swig. "She's hard to talk to since Sammy woke up. That's all that matters to her, anyway."

"What matters to you?"

I hadn't thought about it that way.

"Do you even think they'd listen?" I asked. To be fair, my mother had almost heard me out that afternoon before she got too wild-eyed.

Zoe hefted herself over a twisted series of roots alongside the trail. We were approaching my favorite spot, a stand of young birch, thin trees that moved gently when you pushed the branches aside. Above us, a line of Canada geese was honking over and I could see flashes of their long white bellies through the canopy of green.

"They've been distracted," Zoe said. "But most parents care about their kids enough to want to know what really happened."

The way she said this made me feel both stupid and scared. If my parents didn't care enough to hear my side of the story, what did that mean? I slowed way down, shrugged off my pack, let Zoe move ahead. I leaned against a flat,chipped boulder, familiar, a place our family always stopped on this trail. The boulder rose like a lichen-covered wall and sun came through the birch, dappling the skin on my arm into complex patterns. Sammy loved this hike. I remembered when he was two, my father carried him up the mountain, and Sammy fell asleep on the way down. I had followed them, watching the qualities of light on my brother's face, how his head lolled gently against my father's shoulder with each step. I felt suddenly irritated. Maybe Zoe's family was perfect. How come she never talked about them? Was Phil some wonder dad in disguise?

I called to Zoe's disappearing back, "What about Phil? Does he want to know what you think every minute?"

She turned, saw I was behind her, and came back. She leaned against the rock next to me. I could see a line of sweat inching down her neck, and I held onto my pack straps to keep my fingers from reaching out and wiping it off. "Phil's not my top choice for family," Zoe said mildly. "He's an alcoholic."

"What about your mom? I don't even know if she's alive." I flinched inside as I said it, tasted the meanness.

"She lives in New York City. She's an artist." Zoe palmed a birch trunk the diameter of her arm, flicking the paper skin that had begun to peel, didn't look at me. It was almost as if she had pulled a shutter closed and I couldn't see behind it. "She visits me in L.A. Sometimes."

"I bet she's coming to Daggett Lake," I said, making it up to her, my voice disgustingly cheerful.

"She may. Or she may be on a trip. She travels a lot." Zoe still wasn't looking at me, but her face flushed suddenly. "I don't even know ahead of time where she's going but she always sends me these cool postcards," she said, each word coming fast. "From India. Japan. Kamchatka."

"Where's that? Sounds far away."

"Russia," she said. "Russia is very far away."

"Oh," I said. We were silent for a minute.

"What's your mom like? Does she have red hair too?"

Her breathing slowed. "Yeah. Pretty wild. She's not your idea of a regular mother. She never made cookies. But she sang me lullabies she made up, on the spot."

"My mother sang me lullabies too. French ones. Off-key."

"My mother has a great voice. Once she sent me this tape of songs she'd recorded. Just for me."

"Why don't you live with her?"

"I told you." She sounded irritated again. "She travels. She can't take care of a kid."

Zoe was talking about escape. I knew all about this. I still watched my mother for signs of it, when she was too still, when she chafed against my father's yearning. But she was home most nights now. She didn't ever go to places like Kamchatka.

I stared toward the range of mountains around us, trying to imagine what it was like for my mother to live with my dad when he became so full of his art he didn't care if anyone else was alive. I wondered if she saw the good parts that Anna talked about, and that's why she came back to him: his love for Sammy in the series of small sketches, his aching response to beauty.

Zoe stroked the trunk of the birch tree with one long finger. I watched her face, wondered if her mother, in Russia or Japan, knew how beautiful her daughter was. Zoe's head was bent now, her sneaker carving a hole in the dirt by the twist of tree roots, disturbing a clump of feathery fern.

So I bent too, stilled her foot, and picked the fern, delicate, fronds still curled into tiny fists, the air around it full of green tang, the essence of the Adirondack woods. I twirled the fern between my fingers for a few seconds then handed it to her, not knowing why.

She took it and finally looked up, her eyes full of tears. I knew about those tears. Things lost, especially hope.

The next step was easy. I held out my arms.

I gathered Zoe in.

For long moments, we stayed like that. I felt the wetness on my shoulder, the twitching of her body, occasional movements like a small animal rutting against its mother, seeking comfort. I held her quietly, the light shifting slowly on the path between us. Far below, a truck passed on the road. A motorboat started up. I felt a few drops of rain on my arm, carrying balsam scent from the summit.

Finally Zoe's silent crying stopped. In slow motion, she pulled herself away, and I immediately missed the heat of her against me. She wiped her face on one sleeve of the silver shirt, not embarrassed at all, and I liked that. We looked at each other, not sure what to do next. Her lips opened a little as she finished cleaning her face. I saw her eyes drop to my mouth.

I leaned forward. It was an easy motion, as if my body almost expected it, as if it were the most natural decision I could make.

It wasn't earthshaking, for a first kiss. But it was different. Chad's lips had been firm, like the skin on someone's arm, scratchy from the edge of beard growth on his chin. Zoe's lips were as soft as the moss that surrounded the tiny fern I'd just plucked for her. But what I really loved was the slowness. Her kiss was languid and easy, like we had all the time in the world.

It started a hum in my heart, and as I kissed her back, the hum got louder.

Above us, someone whistled sharp for a dog. We broke apart, startled. I felt behind me, regaining my balance against the rock. We were in full view of practically anyone. My face heated and I quickly looked for my daypack, began to buckle it on. Her voice stopped me.

"Molly?"

She was smiling at me, her eyes searching. They were clear, unshuttered now, and I strained inside, wanting that question, just as the part of me that was scared pulled back. I opened my mouth to say, "It's Okay," but the words swam away before my lips could form them. So I just stood there, trying to smile, trying not to cry.

"Thank you," she said. "I mean it."

The dog barked again and the person laughed. Zoe picked up her pack, turned, and began walking up the path. I followed.

Walking became dancing, more than just placing one foot

before another. I watched the swing of her hips toward the top of the mountain and sensed again the welcome lightness and tension in my body.

Ahead were warm rocks to lie on, sun-sparkled lake below. I felt like I'd be able to fly if I wanted to. I could leap across the foothills to Whiteface Mountain.

I knew on a day like this it would be clear as anything in the distance.

Chapter 29

The heat was more intense on the summit, although a few of the mountains around us were cottony with cloud wisps. Zoe went immediately to a shady spot by a cluster of pines. She sat, pulling off her pack, and I settled near her, wondering what either of us would say about what had just happened. But she didn't say anything.

The fern was still in her hand. She just placed it on the rock between us like a bookmark.

She began looking in her backpack, pulling out an apple, a knife and napkins she'd packed. She held up the apple like an offering.

"Want some?"

I nodded.

She cut it, scooped out the black seeds, handed half to me. It was tart and tasted as good as it smelled. Sweat was tickling the back of my neck and I wiped it off, lifted my face as a breeze came and the pines moved. First their tops rustled then the lower branches, then the grasses near our knees. The breeze smelled like everything I loved about mountains: rain and sun, grass and trees, lichen and flowers.

Behind us sat the family with the dog. They were clumped helter-skelter on another rockface, laughing at one of the little kids and his shrill, excited, rambling story about a bear. He was obviously getting it wrong and his older sister leapfrogged over him with kind correction, the parents adding their bits. The dog barked happily.

Zoe was smiling at this too. She began searching in her pack again. "Close your eyes," she told me, and I felt something smooth on my palm.

"Okay, now look."

It was a rock shaped like a little fish.

"What's this for?"

"It's rose quartz. I bought it for you."

The fish had a notch for the eyes, a little slit for the mouth. I turned it over in my hand, liking the shape, the feel. It stared up at me, almost joyous.

"I got it at the health food store in Saranac. It's supposed to be healing when a person's really sad." She was studying my face. "The fish means coming out of dark places, like diving into water then coming up different. But Okay." She frowned, trying to remember. "Like how water looks lighter closer to the surface. Do you like it?"

Diving for Sammy's body, I hadn't noticed any light in the water, but Chad had talked about it in his dreams. Surfacing into light sounded good, wholesome.

"There's another thing. See this symbol?" Zoe turned the quartz to reveal a tiny mark in the side. "Peril and opportunity, the Chinese character for change. Change is sad sometimes because it's like going into dark." She picked up a paper napkin and polished the side of the quartz, held it so I could see the faint etching. "But there's always light too."

Behind us was a sudden flurry of movement. The family of hikers, the two kids and the big black dog, were packing up. We watched them head down the mountain in a ragged line, their noisy chatter fading into the distance.

In the aftermath of silence and light summit wind, Zoe leaned toward me. She placed the palm of one hand against my face for a few seconds. Her hand was smooth and warm.

The gesture was so tender, so unexpected, it startled me more than the kiss. It felt like she was touching more than just my skin, like she was holding something in that threatened to crack and spill out.

"I don't really know what's happening to me." My voice came out very small.

"Neither do I," she said. "But isn't that Okay?"

I'd never seen her look so vulnerable. I nodded.

She smiled at me and stood up, brushing her hands on her shorts.

"I'm starving. We should go down this mountain and get two of Lester's grease burgers. Maybe three. What do you think about that?"

She stood in front of me, hands on her hips, daring me to object.

"And fries?" I said.

"Don't forget your fish," Zoe said.

I palmed the rose quartz. I made sure to slide it in the pocket that didn't have the new jackknife.

Chapter 30

When I woke up different the next morning, at first I didn't know what the difference was. I took inventory as I lay under the thin sheet, watching light play on the birch leaves outside the screen of my sleeping porch. The early sun always striped the trunks a rose gold, and the light always made me feel optimistic, like something bad could have passed while I slept. Then I realized it was true. Fear was absent from my body for the first time since the accident.

I thought of the talismans under my pillow and felt for them. They were all there, nestled in warmth: Sammy's fire engine, the puzzle piece and the stone fish from Zoe. I made my bed without disturbing them.

Around ten, my father came back from the hospital, went over to the sink, and swept my mother into his arms. I continued to eat my breakfast, but my mouth was open, watching my parents dance in the kitchen.

"We can see your cereal, Molly." But my mother was giggling as she said this because my father bent her backward in a swoop, ending the tango. He set her upright and her face was flushed and happier than I'd see it in months.

Enthusiasm was all over the small room. "Sammy's coming home," I guessed.

"Bingo." My mother grinned at me. "Isn't that super?"

"This Saturday," my father added. "Day after tomorrow." He was almost smiling at me, like everything was suddenly forgiven. Despite his excellent mood, I was irritated.

"He's really Okay? You're sure?" I asked.

"He's woken up for good," my mother said. "He's really Okay."

I took my cereal bowl to the sink and ran water over it, paralyzed by a new fear. What had my brother said in his sleepy waking moments? How he hated his sister Molly? That she'd shown off in the boat and caused everything to go wrong on his birthday?

"Did Sam say anything, when he woke up?"

My mother grinned. "He said, *Mommy, I'm starving.*"

I faced my father, ignoring the warning in his eyes, enunciating every word. "Anything else?"

"No."

"The doctors are sure he won't fall back asleep?"

My mother laughed lightly, her hands moving uneasily against the front of her shirt. "I certainly hope so. Everyone needs sleep."

"Molly means, will he fall asleep again and not wake up." My dad watched me over the rim of his new blue mug as if he knew why I was asking all these questions.

Tension in my chest tightened as I watched him breathe. We were in some kind of struggle, visible just to us two, and my mother could only look on, bewildered and slightly annoyed.

My father set his mug down. "Sam woke up this morning." His words were simple, as precise as mine had been. "He's hungry. He's talking a bit, not a lot. They've started testing. They'll know more tomorrow. The doctor's optimistic."

"We all are." As if to emphasize her certainty, my mother went over to my father and wrapped her arms around his waist. Her hair was braided too, but in one silvery rope that hung against my father's tanned arm. They stood entwined in an unfamiliar unity, watching me.

"Good," I said finally. "I'm really glad Sammy's coming home Saturday. Can we have a welcome home party?"

"I'm going to the studio," my father said. "You girls work it out. Kate, are you off to the hospital soon?"

"After I shower. Molly, you come too. Sammy asked for you."

Her words made me instantly happy. And terrified.

Sammy was sitting up in bed. I waved to him, relief sweeping me. From the doorway, he looked the same. But as I got closer, I saw his eyes were different. I set down my backpack slowly, walked toward the bed.

"Meemee?"

My breath came out in a whoosh. Recognition and love. I could see both in his face.

"Hi, Sammy Sam. I missed you."

He shivered. "It's so cold in here."

"I can fix that," I said, grateful to do something for him, forestall the questions and blame.

I let my mother drop her bags in a chair and hug Sammy first, while I located the room's thermostat. "How are you feeling, Sammy?"

"He's wonderful." My mother's voice was muffled in Sammy's back. She was rocking him, his head limp against her shoulder, rolling easily with the familiar motion.

"I'm wonderful," he said. "Can I have some toast?"

I turned off the air conditioning and found an extra blanket. When my mother put Sammy back in bed, I draped the blanket over his legs. I noticed he was thinner than before the accident when I went to hug him, but his arms around my neck were surprisingly strong.

"You are wonderful. What have they been feeding you?" A stupid thing to ask. He wouldn't know. I squeezed tighter, stepped back. "I know. You've been lifting weights in your sleep."

He giggled at that. Held up the lion. "Meet Leo."

"Good name," I said. "How about the others?"

"I don't know." His smile came briefly, watery, then he frowned at the lion.

I ruffled his hair. "We gotta get you a haircut, kiddo."

He swatted my hand away. "Stop it. I hate that." Then he twisted away, his voice plaintive. "Mom, I have to go to the bathtub."

On the Internet site Chad showed me, I'd read about this. How sometimes a person got circuits scrambled after a head injury. Their words, their speech. Anything could happen. But my mother didn't know this. Her body stilled and her busy hands fell to her sides.

"What, love?" She went toward Sammy, but he flailed his little arms, thin as sticks.

"I've got to go, Mama."

My mother opened her mouth, then shook her head and pressed the nurse's call button. When a cheerful redhaired woman appeared, she said, "My son has to use the bathroom. Do I take him?"

The nurse's apple cheeks stretched in a big smile aimed at Sammy. "It's your first visit together. Why don't you just relax while we take care of business?" She walked over to the bed and deftly moved the IV bag onto a rolling pole with a hook in the top. Bent down to pull back Sammy's blankets, including the one I'd added, reached lower to help Sammy put one, then the other foot on the floor. He clung to her arm, easy with her, almost unmoving. They shuffled toward the small bathroom and the door closed.

I could hear her murmuring, encouraging, the tinkle of urine into the toilet, his voice too low for any words, the flush. My mother and I didn't move, just stood listening until they emerged, Sammy walking steadily, the nurse trailing a few steps behind him with the IV pole rolling silently.

My mother's face looked fierce. "I brought you some books, Sammy. Would you like to see them?"

He settled himself against the bed pillows. "Read to me?"

"I can," I said. I wanted to read to Sammy more than anything. My mother pulled a book at random from the stack.

"Shall I bring some juice for everybody?" said the nurse. "Sammy likes pineapple."

Sammy never liked pineapple.

"Okay," I said. I pulled the straight-backed chair as close as possible against the bed. On the shelf where the animals sat was Chad's iPod.

"Excuse me." My mother was following the nurse out of the room. "Can I talk with you for a minute?"

The book was *The Berenstain Bears.* We'd read it a million times. "Do you want to sing to me instead?"

He looked up at my face. "I don't know any songs." Frowning, "Do I?"

I took a deep breath to get my heart to start again and opened the book. Sister Bear was in trouble. "You used to read this yourself. Do you want to sit up and tell me the story while I turn the pages?"

Sammy shook his head, thumb in his mouth, leaned against the stack of pillows. His eyes were half closed. I looked at him for a minute, studying the soft cheek. Then I reached into my pocket for the rose quartz fish Zoe had given me. I placed it in Sammy's other hand, the one curled limply on the blanket between us. He brought it close to his face, turning it over and studying the design on the side. Then he handed it back to me and closed his eyes completely.

I began to read.

Chapter 31

After steady rain for three days, nobody could get used to the sun. Least of all Sammy, whose eyes had been closed since early summer. When we brought him home from the hospital, he was still blinking a lot, so my mother bought him a pair of sunglasses as cool as Chad's.

Chad met us when we drove in, the four of us in the station wagon, my father driving, my mother singing, the windows open. I sat in the back with Sammy and tried not to notice how quiet he was during the ride, how upset he got when my father went over a bump too fast, how he started crying when his cherry popsicle ran down his arms.

For some reason I wasn't all that surprised. It was almost a relief that everything wasn't perfect like my mother said it would be. But I could see how stricken she was. How my father's cheeriness felt so strange, it was a strain to hear his voice. So I sat in the back and mopped up my brother, sang old camp songs—*She'll be coming round the mountain, Kumbaya, Hope you live to be a hundred*—laughed at my father's lame jokes, and generally tried to keep spirits up, buffer everyone else's emotions. Mine were way too outrageous.

By the time we bumped over another pothole and pulled into the parking area, Sammy's mouth was turned down in another scowl and I was exhausted. Seeing Chad Anderson didn't help.

He walked up to the car, his hands in the pockets of his khakis, the sunglasses dangling from a neon strap around his neck. He had gotten a haircut. He smiled at me.

"Chad," said my mother, as if they were best friends. "Want to help unload stuffed animals?"

"Those are mine," Sammy said. He clambered out of the car, blinking in the light of the parking meadow, tugging at the tail of his Superman shirt.

"Hi, kid," Chad said. "Nice to see you up and about." He came over and put an arm around me. I tried to shrug it off then remembered this was the person responsible for Sammy standing here, awake and alive and back with us.

"You remember Chad, from next door?" I said.

"Hi," Sammy said. "Are you Molly's boyfriend?"

"No," I said. I handed him his iPod.

Chad took his arm away and stuffed the iPod in his pocket. He picked up two bags my mother had packed with stuffed animals.

"Let's get Leo down to the cabin, show him around," I said. I grabbed the other bag and took Sammy's hand.

Jays were darting through the clearing, calling. It was one of those beautiful days we rarely got in late July, when the air started to cool toward August and the humidity dropped. A sheaf of maple leaves in a tree high above us was already edged with red.

My brother walked carefully, peering down the front of his blue cargo shorts, staring at the ground like he'd never seen it before. Once he stumbled and I held him up. We dropped the bag of animals on the cabin steps and I started to go inside, but Sammy tugged at me. "The lake, Meemee. I remember. Isn't there a big rock?"

"Where you liked to sit." This remembering made me feel warm and happy.

"Let's go there," he said.

I looked behind us. "We should ask Mom."

My parents came up the steps, my father laden with hospital plants.

"Sammy wants to see the lake."

My father frowned at me. I grasped Sammy's hand tighter.

"Maybe we should have lunch first." Mom's voice was high. "Sammy, do you want a hot dog?"

"I wanna go to the rock!"

Inside the cabin the phone began ringing. "That could be Anna," my mother said. "Nobody move." She went in to answer. "Molly! It's for you."

Sammy was looking like he would cry any second. "Can you wait, kiddo?" I said. "The rock will be there in a few minutes. We'll all go down."

Chad reached for Sammy's hand. "I could take him down there, Mrs. Fisher."

"I'm coming," my mother said. "Let me get a sweater." She disappeared back inside. As I followed her, I heard Sammy say, "I heard a song when I was asleep."

"I know," said Chad. He was dressed up again today, in khakis and a red polo shirt, as if he were expecting company. I held the screen door, listening.

"It told me to wake up."

I started to move forward, to tell him it had been my idea to play the music. But Sammy coughed and looked up at Chad. "Are you my friend?"

"That's right," Chad said.

Zoe was on the phone. "How'd it go?" she asked.

"I can't really talk right now." I was keeping an eye on Chad and Sammy and my mother through the window of the cabin, their careful progress down the dirt path, their disappearance toward the lake. My father was banging around on the screen porch, getting out balloons, the welcome-home sign we hadn't had time to put up earlier.

"Is your brother still acting weird?" Zoe asked.

"More than ever."

"Like what kinds of things?"

I could hear voices in the background. "Where are you calling from?"

"Phil wanted to get a beer, so we're at the Boat House. He's getting totally wasted."

"Chad's family is away. Maybe you could stay there."

"It may not be an issue," Zoe said. "There's a woman smiling at Phil. I just have to get him in her car."

"Maybe Lester will help." I peered out the window. I couldn't see my brother or Chad or my mother. "I have to go." I hung up fast.

On the float, about twenty yards from where Chad and Sammy sat, was a family of Merganser ducks. Cute, with fuzzy head feathers, they were happily covering our diving board with poop, chattering away to each other. Chad waved to me as I approached, putting a finger to his lips.

I tiptoed up, touched my brother's hair. He started.

"Meemee," he said, his voice loud.

The ducks looked up. One by one they began lowering themselves into the water and swimming away.

"Nonono," Sammy called. "Don't leave, ducks." He turned, frowning at me. "You were noisy."

"I was quiet," I said. "You were the one who called my name."

"I did *not*." He stood up, his hands on his little hips.

My mother, reading on the dock, looked at us, her face full of alarm.

"Molly ruined everything," Sammy said and burst into tears.

It was a great welcome home. My mother made me sit on the dock, with Chad, and she moved to the rock and held Sammy. He cried and pounded on her legs with his little fists.

Finally he called over to me, "Meemee!" as if nothing had happened. I went to the rock, and Chad and I sat there while Sammy let me put my arm around him. My mother went back to the dock to read.

Eventually he lay down in my lap, his head on my legs, and fell asleep.

"Jiggle him a little," Chad said softly, not wanting my mother to hear.

I shifted slightly on the rock. Sammy's eyes opened. "Meemee?" He yawned, huge.

"It's Okay," I said. I smoothed the hair on his forehead and he didn't bat me away, just smiled and closed his eyes.

I shifted again, a tiny movement of legs. Sammy stirred, murmured like anyone would, but didn't open his eyes.

"He's really different," Chad said.

I nodded. "Right after a person wakes up, it's sometimes worse. Did you know that?"

"No," Chad said. "I didn't know if he was going to wake up."

We watched Sammy breathing. His face was flushed, eyes moving under his seashell lids. After a while, Chad got to his feet. "Parents are calling at four to make sure I'm brushing my teeth."

"Where are they?"

"Vegas."

"So you get the cabin all to yourself."

"Not much I want to do all by myself." Chad gave me that look I was beginning to recognize. I stared out at the lake. "Okay," he said. "I'll see you around. Will you be at the Boat House later?"

Sammy was snoring lightly, drooling onto my leg. I shook my head. "Too much family stuff. Mom bought a cake." I wondered if Sammy would remember the lack of cake on his birthday. Or remember his birthday at all. I thought of the hospital room, Sammy wanting to go to the bathtub instead of the bathroom.

Chad stepped off the big rock, straightened his shirttail until it hung evenly over the pressed khakis. Pushed up his glasses. Waited.

"Thanks," I said.

He nodded. Then he turned and walked down the shoreline path that separated our cabins.

Chapter 32

After dinner, Sammy opened presents and greeted his animals. My parents were so hopeful, their faces so expectant, I did everything I could to make the evening fun for Sammy, to keep him from one of his new fits of anger. When he started crying, not finding Leo right away, I remembered we left him by the rock. By the time I ran back up the hill, Sammy was smiling again.

By eight, his bed was ready for him and he was sleepy. We all trooped in to get him into his pajamas, watch him brush his teeth. It wasn't even dark yet. My parents hovered, my father straightening books on the bedside shelf and checking the screen to make sure it was tight. But other than waking him every few minutes all night long, there was nothing we could do to make sure Sammy would be with us in the morning. So we let him fall asleep.

My mother brushed the hair from my brother's forehead. "He's home," she whispered. "That's what matters." She walked out of the bedroom and soon I heard dishes clattering in the kitchen.

My father and I stayed for a few more minutes. "It'll be Okay," I said. "We'll see him in the morning."

Sammy murmured in his sleep and I saw my father smile. His face looked softer in the evening light.

My parents went down to the dock after the dishes were done. I agreed to stay in the cabin, listen for Sammy if he called. "We won't be that long," my mother said, but I told her to take her time. I wanted to make a phone call.

Zoe answered on the first ring. "I wasn't sure you'd call," she said.

"I had to wait until everyone was busy, or asleep."

"Who's asleep?" she asked. Then, "Oh, yeah, your brother. Is that Okay?"

"He has to sleep." I could hear something clinking in the background, like china being stacked. "Are you doing the dishes?"

"Phil left this total mess." The sound of water came through the phone, another clink. "Before he got drunk, his fishing buddies were here for breakfast."

"Is he gone?"

There was a crash and Zoe swore. "I dropped one of Lester's mugs."

"Probably for the best."

"I'll tell Phil it got broken by one of his friends. He won't remember. He's so mixed up, he's talking about staying after the summer."

My chest cramped suddenly. I inched a slow breath past the cramp into my lungs.

"I'd have to switch schools for my senior year. But there are many other advantages to the idea."

I found my voice. "Party line, Zoe."

"Oh, yeah." There was a long silence. "Hey, anybody listening?"

"Are you going to the Boat House tomorrow night?" I asked. "Chad said he was."

"Boring," Zoe said. "I have another idea."

My mother and father came up from the dock, my mother's face a little flushed. "Let's do the puzzle," she said. "I'll make cocoa. Molly?"

"I want to read in my room." I wanted to watch Sammy sleep.

My mother smiled a little, joined my father at the puzzle table. I felt a new, if uneasy, peace around them, a possibility that hadn't been there before the accident. To celebrate, I slipped into my room and found the piece of blue sky under my pillow.

I returned it back into the pile on the table when my parents weren't looking. Then I went back to my room and listened for hours to my brother's steady breathing.

Chapter 33

When I woke, it was just six. Sam was still asleep but my mother was already up.

"Good morning, early bird," she said, when I walked into the kitchen. Her eyes look rested and still. She was wearing a lemon yellow shift that made her look tall and tan, stirring something that smelled like oranges and cinnamon. "Sleep Okay?"

"I saw the sunrise from my bed. There's mist all over the lake this morning. Are you making breakfast?"

"Two kinds of muffins," my mother said. "And frittata. Sammy's welcome home." She added an egg to the bowl. Onions sizzled on the stove, and my mother covered the skillet with a tin pie plate. She sighed.

"We could start over," I said. "Get all new pans."

"Nobody would notice except you and me." We smiled at each other. "Would you like some hot tea?" she said. "You look a little chilled."

I wasn't really chilly. I was warmed by the changes happening to all of us, filling up emptiness in an unexpected way. Now that

Sam was awake, I could let myself wonder if the accident would set us all on a new track.

I sat in a chair by the tiny kitchen table. The early sun was coming in through the trees, just the first faint lines of it, and the window was open a little, letting in the smell of the woods. The suncatcher in the window spun easily.

"Did he wake up in the night?"

"I came in around midnight. You both were asleep. Then he woke at two. Did you hear us?" She frowned a little. "He said something really odd when I took him to the bathroom."

"It's the coma, Mom. He gets words mixed up." I reached for the mug and almost dropped it. The tea was scalding.

"No, this was different." She paused, thinking. "He said, *Did you find my jackknife?* No. *Does Molly have my jackknife?* That was it."

The pie plate over the onions rattled in a tiny burst of steam.

"Those are burning," I said.

My mother bent over the skillet and sniffed. "They're fine." She lowered the heat.

My mug had left a steam ring on the surface of the kitchen table and I played with it, pushing the circle outward with one finger until it broke. "Maybe he was dreaming," I said.

She rinsed the yellow bowl, laid it on a kitchen towel to drain, wiped her hands on her jeans, and poured more coffee into a blue mug.

"I dreamed about dancing," I offered. "With Sammy. This waltz tune."

The timer went off, one of those homey sounds, and my mother pulled a twelve-hole muffin tin from the oven. They were golden domes flecked with dark blue. She flicked them into a towel-covered basket, brought two pottery plates, knives and the butter to the table. Then sat down, sipped her coffee.

"Blueberries from Catamount," she said. "We picked them last summer. Remember? I'm making orange muffins too."

I spread butter on the hot blueberry-colored dough, watching it melt and steam, trying to get the whole thing to my mouth before it crumbled. There wasn't any talking for a minute.

Then my mother said, "I was putting away some laundry in your room yesterday, Molly."

"I forgot to make my bed yesterday," I said quickly. "Sorry."

My mother waved one hand. "I don't expect you to make your bed. It's summer vacation." She paused. "I found something in your dresser."

The muffin had glued itself to the back of my throat. I grabbed the tea and took a big gulp, burning my tongue.

My mother reached into the pocket of her jeans and set the jackknife on the table. It lay between us, glinting in the kitchen's early morning light. I felt dismayed at the timing of this discovery, when I was so hopeful in the soar of Sammy's homecoming.

My mother stared at the jackknife and so did I. "When Sammy said that funny thing, after I found this . . . " She looked up at me.

I was suddenly tired of it all: the lies, covering for Sam. "I didn't take the jackknife."

My mother pressed the mug to her cheek. "But here it is. Or one just like it."

"Sammy took it. He said Daddy promised to give it to him for his birthday."

My mother snorted. "That wasn't going to happen."

I tensed and she stopped, waiting.

"Sammy had the knife on the boat that day. He fell in because he dropped it in the water. He was leaning to catch it."

The silence was absolute. My mother was holding her coffee mug so tightly I thought her fingers would fuse with the ceramic. She looked like she was sifting through what she loved, the mixed inventory of it, assessing the guilt of each person against her love for that person, and weighing the two. I was sure we would all come up short.

I started to get up, but she placed one palm, warm from her cup, on my forearm. My mother's hand was smooth, the pink oval nails with their white moons an exquisite contrast of familiar and unfamiliar that made my eyes sting.

"Molly," she said slowly, "I know how much you've been taking care of Sammy. But you don't need to anymore. I can help."

Tears were streaking my cheeks. "You're leaving anyway," I

hiccupped. "I heard you tell Aunt Anna."

"I'm right here. I'm not going anywhere."

I didn't believe her. "No one really notices what's going on with Sammy. I tried to tell you about the knife, about what happened."

She sighed. "That knife is truly dangerous. I should've stolen it myself, got rid of it long ago."

Her voice was clear and firm enough to lean on. "I got rid of it for you," I whispered. "It's at the bottom of the lake. Nobody has to know."

"That's not good enough." My mother was taking deep calming breaths, coming to a decision. "Number one, you will tell your father everything." I started to shake my head, but she held up a hand. "It's not negotiable, Molly. He needs to know about the knife, what Sammy did, but also that he was partly responsible. You were too, of course, taking out the boat. But the drama of the jackknife is all his." She handed me a wad of tissues from her jeans pocket. "These are clean."

I mopped my face. "What's number two?"

"Your brother needs to stop stealing things, and you need to stop covering for him. If we're to get stronger and love each other again, this family can't handle those kinds of secrets."

I looked over at her portrait on the main room wall, the only live image surrounded by still objects, my dad's attempt to capture her unending flight. Her lips were parted, her unshadowed eye slightly amused, as if she knew the futility of his action. She followed my gaze.

"Your father and I do love each other. We're just different in how we love. The accident taught me about that."

"I knew you were going to leave, Mom."

She shook her head, her eyes steady and clear. I don't think she'd ever looked as beautiful or as certain. "I'm not going anywhere, Molly. You don't have to worry about that. In a good marriage, everyone gives up a little. Something you'll learn when you fall in love."

I wondered what I would give up.

My mother took a final sip of her coffee and set the cup down.

She pointed to the knife. "Tell me where that one came from."

"Anna found it in Willsboro."

My mother turned it over delicately. "It's amazingly like Willie's."

"It's not really, but it's from the same war."

She nodded, accepting my knowledge. She was rotating it slowly in one small hand, reading the engraving on the side.

I asked carefully, "What do you know about Willie?"

"Only that something happened between them before Willie died. I don't know the whole story, although I think Anna does. Sometimes I think Willie and your father were more than just good friends. War can do that, bring people close."

It was strange, knowing more than my mother. I thought of Willie, an imagined face, bodies in the dark. The yearning low in my belly when Zoe kissed me.

"How did Willie die?"

"An explosion. Your father was lucky. He was injured but not very much, just enough to come home right after. Willie didn't make it." My mother shook her head. "I think your father's injury happened inside. He's a very complex person."

"He's a very simple person when he's mad," I said glumly. "And he'll really be mad when I tell him Willie's jackknife is at the bottom of the lake."

"He loves you. That will win out."

I hoped so. I hoped it would for all of us.

"I'll let him know you have something important to tell him. That'll make it easier."

We sat for a minute. My voice was still low, trembly from crying so hard. I brought out my final unspoken worry, laid it on the table. "Sammy's not right, Mom."

She was silent. "It just takes a while for all the pieces in the brain to reconnect. We just have to be patient."

"How long? Weeks?" I asked, although I knew the answer. I'd done my own research. I just wanted to be sure we all knew.

"Years. We'll make certain he gets help."

My mother stood up and held me there beside the table, took my face in both hands so gently I thought I would start crying again. "It wasn't all your fault. You need to tell your father that."

Eventually my body stopped shaking. She let me go and gathered the plates and her coffee mug. I put the jackknife in my pocket. We heard light footsteps padding across the living room, the bathroom door closing. "Promise me?" she said.

"All right."

The toilet flushed. Sammy appeared in the doorway to the kitchen. He was wearing pajamas with big red stars on them and little sheepskin bedroom slippers no bigger than my hand. His blond hair stuck up in at least three places. He looked like someone had planted flags on his summit. My mother and I both grinned at him. He rubbed his eyes, as if he were trying to get oriented.

"Sammy Sam," I said. He looked at me and his face relaxed. Then he looked at my mother.

"Good morning, honey," she said. She walked over to the doorway, scooped him up in a bear hug, landing kisses all over his rumpled hair, her yellow dress bending toward him like a streak of sunlight. "You sleep well?"

Sammy nodded. "I   smell." he thought for a minute, "muffins . . . ?"

"We saved some for you."

I held up a plateful to show him then lifted it higher. He shuffled toward me, his slippers sliding on the floor. He reached me and the muffins at the same time. I was holding that plate like the Statue of Liberty, my body flushed with relief and gratitude. He wasn't the same but he was here, alive, and that was good beyond words.

Chapter 34

Zoe called to remind me about our date that night. She was waiting when I got to the dock. The sun was down and the sky had a purple glow.

I just could see her face in the darkening light.

"Sammy's Okay?" she said.

I had told her on the phone about the talk with my mother, about what Sam had said. "He's fast asleep, in a good way."

"Awesome." Zoe smiled, her teeth white, her eyes happy for me. She grabbed my hand, hoisted herself to her feet. "Now come see my idea."

She led me off the dock, down the path toward Chad's cabin. I noticed her backpack. "Are we staying awhile?" I said, trying not to trip over tree roots in the dimness. Ahead was a yellow porch light.

"Just some things we'll need," she said mysteriously. "What's that you brought?"

I held up the rusty junk store hurricane light I'd grabbed from the porch. A box of safety matches. "Some things we'll need."

Zoe smiled. Her face, so tan in the daylight, was pale as the sky, her red hair almost black in the dimness. She found my hand, squeezed a little. I tripped over a root at the shock of her skin, and she yanked me up.

"Good thing I wore sneakers," I said.

"His parents are still out of town, yes?" We had reached the porch steps. "And they leave it unlocked?" Zoe asked me.

"Yes. Why?"

"How long does Chad stay at the Boat House these days?"

"Till Lester kicks him out." Probably because I was ignoring his suggestions to be my boyfriend, if the band was rocking, Chad danced all night with any girl he could grab. It made Sarah insane.

Zoe ran up the steps and plopped down in one of the chairs, shrugging off her backpack.

"Why didn't we stay at the dock?" I said, taking the chair next to her, scooting as close as possible.

"Secret surprise. I told you." She leaned back, reached over for my hand again. "Isn't this better? More private?"

The dock was plenty private, I thought. And I'd had enough of secrets this summer. Secrets caused accidents. It was safer being on our dock, and unless the moon was bright, nobody could see us sitting there. Chad's parents left the light on all the time, and although it was on the far end of the porch, I could see the angles of Zoe's cheekbones, the sharp chin. I studied her profile against the pine trees and wooden railings, wondering what her secret was.

"Girls in love need privacy." She smiled at my quick exhale, the shock of her words, and turned to face me. "You know that, Molly?"

It was only when she leaned to kiss me that her hand let go of mine and began tracing lines down the skin on my forearm. Every line was a new tremble, like a mini-earthquake breaking up all that had been frozen inside me, from the summer's darkness. I was melting under the heat of her and I welcomed it like sun after a long Adirondack winter.

This close to the lake, there was the lap of water on rocks.

Night birds every now and then, a hoot in the distance. Voices from the neighboring camps, and occasionally the warble of a loon looking for its mate. But mostly, I heard our breathing. At first I was embarrassed. But when I listened, I noticed Zoe's breathing was fast too.

My eyes were closed, but even in the dark, light played against my inner lids, flashes of color I'd never seen before.

I was used to making my own images, from books and what I saw at school or in the wilderness where we lived. I researched stuff on the Internet, but my family didn't own a television set. It never bothered me or made me think I was missing out, even when all the kids in school talked about the latest sitcom or that hot band on MTV. I was a painter and Okay with that. My parents knew lots of gay artists but they always seemed dramatic and hard to talk to. Not like Zoe. Leaning against her now, I was suddenly aware of how much I didn't know. My models for falling in love were characters like Anna Karenina who made terrible choices and killed herself. I now knew about Willie, but he was an unformed image in my mind. None of the books I was reading for Advanced English talked about women loving other women. You were best friends, yes. You put your arms around each other and shared lipstick. Not lips.

Lips were everything, I discovered now. Lips translated everything, until tongues took over and I had to close my eyes again as the conversation got louder and louder in the silence of breathing and small body noises.

I'd spent hours reliving that first kiss, the one I'd given and gotten on Cloud Lake Mountain. I could still smell the air and dusty rock, feel the mix of tears and sweat on Zoe's face. But that kiss was not like this one.

"Sweet," Zoe whispered, and it was sweet, like liquid dark chocolate. When we finally separated, Zoe cupped my head and brought it toward her shoulder. There I rested, my pulse hammering in my throat.

I couldn't even feel my legs.

Eventually she stood up, took my hand, laughing, tried to pull me to my feet, but I stumbled like an idiot and that made her laugh more. "I brought us a picnic," she said. "Let's go inside."

It had gotten dark enough so the lake was a silvery blur in front of us, the mountains the deepest blue, the shoreline a jagged edge of pine treetops against the evening sky. The first stars had begun to wink, and I could see the bright flash of Venus. The bugs humming around the porch light faded as we walked into the main room.

Chad's cabin was laid out like ours, a great room in the center with a fireplace, separate sleeping porches off the two sides, a long front porch with Adirondack chairs. Zoe brought out a blanket, shook it onto the floor and smoothed the edges. I found a lamp and turned it on. Behind me I heard the clink of china. She was on her knees, carefully folding napkins into triangles, trying to get them to stand up on the plates like we were in a fancy restaurant. She reached into the backpack for iced tea, a long loaf of bread, a knife that glinted in the lamplight and made me start. Cheese and grapes and a bar of chocolate.

She got to her feet. "Madame?" She bowed low from the waist. "Dinner is served."

Close up, the picnic was Lester's chipped mugs and two plastic red plates, but Zoe poured iced tea into the mugs like they were fine crystal. "To us," she said. "Long may we reign."

"Over what?" I said, finding my voice.

"Does it matter?" she said, sipping from the mug. "Sit down, girl."

I sat, let her fill my plate with grapes and Vermont cheddar, chunks of chocolate and bread sliced from the loaf. All good, except the iced tea.

"Instant," she said, seeing my face.

"Everything else is good." Why were we talking about food?

She pressed her palms together, like she was holding hands with herself. "We're good. We fit like this. I've never met anyone like you."

I took care with my piece of cheese, breaking it up and smashing it into the bread. "I'm not that special," I said, my mouth full.

"How do you know?" Zoe said. She reached for a grape, brought it to her mouth. I could see her hand was trembling. "You kiss like a dream."

I was glad she was nervous too, glad the light was behind me and she couldn't see my face. "I don't," I said.

"You do."

"And you should know?" I swallowed the last bit of bread. "How many people have you kissed?"

Zoe shook her head and I remembered the trembling fingers. "You think I'm this experienced person, don't you? I'm not Sarah. I don't go around kissing everyone I come into contact with."

"I didn't think that." I busied myself with more bread and cheese.

"But you want to know."

I was silent, chewing.

"I'm only two years older than you. And I've only been with two people."

"Girls?"

"One girl, one guy," Zoe said. "The guy was a mistake." She was studying me. "You ever kiss a girl before?"

"You already asked me that."

"And you didn't answer."

"I haven't even kissed very many guys," I said. "I haven't exactly been all that popular."

"You're gorgeous." She said this quietly, a fact.

My skin tingled. "Not really," I said. But I wanted to say, Really? I was gorgeous? She was the gorgeous one, the talented water-skier that everyone on the lake was talking about because she could make a circle of plywood ride across the surface like walking on water.

"Yes, really. I think about you all the time." She shrugged. "It makes me crazy."

I was incredulous. "You make *me* crazy. Ever since I first saw you, that day in the Boat House. With all those guys drooling over you."

We grinned silly at each other, then we both turned to look out the windows at the lake. The cicadas were louder now. It was still warm from the day, from the welcome sunshine, but there was a breeze off the water that felt good on my overheated skin. It didn't cool me inside.

Zoe began gathering up the picnic, dumping the plates and mugs into a plastic bag, folding the blanket carefully, setting it by her backpack. "Now for my secret surprise," she said. "If you're not feeling chicken."

"I'm not chicken about much." A big lie. "I like surprises." Another lie.

"Then take off your shirt."

"My shirt?"

"A massage." She pulled a bottle out of the side pocket of the pack and held it up, but her eyes looked unsure. "You can give me one afterward. I read about how to do it in that magazine of Sarah's." When I didn't move, she added, "Only if you want to."

I was scared enough to notice my mouth was completely dry and sweat tingled down my back. I knew it was a moment, like crossing into another country. "Of course I do," I said firmly. I briefly reviewed the bra I'd chosen to wear, then before I could change my mind, I pulled my shirt over my head.

"Your bra too," Zoe said. "It'll make it easier."

It wasn't easier for me. In fact, my pulse accelerated until I was sure she could see the rhythm in my throat. But I flicked the bra clasp open, held the limp straps under my arms, turned my back to her.

From behind me, she lifted my glasses off my face, folding them neatly and putting them near her pack. Her hands touched my shoulders, warm hands, palms rough from days in the water. They spread over my skin, inching the bra straps down until they met the resistance of my arms. I let the sides of the bra slide down to my waist, the straps still hanging on my forearms until I let them go too.

Without my glasses, the world blurred completely. Even the small definitions that made moonlight and darkness were gone. All that was left was sound and touch. I heard the click of a bottle top, the slurp of something pouring. When it touched my skin, traveling on her hands to my shoulders, I shivered once. "Be still," she said. "They say it feels better if you relax."

I really tried. Eventually the language her hands were speaking to my skin permeated my brain and I began to breathe into each stroke. It wasn't relaxing at all.

Once, her hands working my sides brushed the edges of my breasts and the melting surged into parts that weren't being massaged. I imagined myself as a large amoebic form without any edges, each cell connected in some indescribable way to other cells, each translating touch. To the lowest part of my back at the waist of my jeans she dove with her hands, then worked her way back up to my shoulders and arms. She held my arm out straight to my side, massaged each finger of each hand from its base to its tip. Smoothed my skin like she smoothed the tablecloth for our picnic, getting all the wrinkles out.

My father once told me about a painting assignment his teacher gave him in grad school. She brought in a basket of folded slips of paper, a feeling written on each. Each student picked one slip, then painted the word on it. I liked the idea. Last summer I wrote myself a basket of words, reached in, picked *surrender*. That was the summer I began pears. I chose to paint a whole pear, lying on its side on a red cloth, and next to it, a halved pear, open and exposed.

That's how I felt under Zoe's hands. Halved and waiting.

Chapter 35

When she stopped, we both stayed still.

I could hear crickets humming through the screens, bugs frantic around the yellow porch light, but inside where we were, even the air was quiet. Zoe's hands rested on my shoulders, then I felt the heat of them lift off, heard the scritch of her wiping them on her jeans, felt light fingers against my hair. Her voice was low in my ear.

"Lean back against me."

Leaning back meant letting my chest rise, allowing cool air on my breasts. Once Sarah had talked about camping out in the nude with Mark, her description of sunlight on breasts odd and queasy in the telling. But night air on my naked skin was everything sensuous. Zoe's body against my bare back still radiated the day's heat. She pulled my head to her shoulder and ran those fingers through my scalp.

"Like that?"

"I do." We weren't speaking more than in whispers.

"Do you know how to turn off that porch light?"

"By the front door," I guessed.

She leaned me forward and got up. I bent over my knees, cupping myself until the room darkened. I heard her come back and smelled the sharp sulfur of a match. The hurricane candle sputtered then caught.

I would be sixteen in three weeks. By now I should've been used to this. But nobody had touched me where Zoe began exploring in that soft light.

Some night animal rustled loud outside. We both halted. My skin was suddenly so hot I imagined I'd be glowing in the near dark if I opened my eyes.

"Chad?" Zoe whispered urgently.

I shook my head. "A raccoon," I said, and she laughed quietly.

I let out the breath I'd been holding. I started to pull my T-shirt over me, realizing that anyone coming up the steps could see us through the front screens, outlined among the fishing plaques by flickering candlelight. But Zoe's hands began moving again and I didn't care.

Every time I let Chad's face pass across my imagination, or whenever I imagined my mother and father back at the cabin, watching Sammy sleep with his lion, it felt like a story. Like putting something real against the pages of *Anna Karenina*. I couldn't grasp both at the same time. This was real: Zoe's hands, Zoe's whisper in my left ear, the pressing heat of chest on my naked back.

In books, women swooned. When Zoe touched my nipple, I got it totally.

I gasped.

She laughed and held me a little tighter. Her hands told me it meant a lot to her too, this massage turned into more.

"I don't know what I'm supposed to do."

Zoe moved her hands through my hair. "That's the whole point. You're supposed to lean back, let it carry you." She tugged at my arm and I slowly turned. There we were, halfway to completely naked, facing each other.

Zoe's body was blurred without my glasses but lean and strong, arms and shoulders almost sculpted. I saw them when she was skiing, but as part of the whole package they stunned me. Her breasts small, the nipples dark brown. I could see a faint whiteness at the collarbone where her tan stopped. A breeze blew up, bringing the scent of lake through the screens. Goose bumps rose, my nipples tightening into tiny gumdrops. I shivered.

Zoe reached behind us and pulled over floor cushions then the blanket from our picnic. "Here," she said, nudging me until I lifted onto the cushions, pulling the blanket over us, wrapping our bodies so tightly, our breasts pressed toward each other on the makeshift bed.

We lay still for a while, breathing almost in rhythm, fast and waiting.

The night was pitch black now, cool, stars and moon faint through the pine trees. I imagined looking down from the top of the tallest tree, watching our two bodies. Stars would highlight Zoe's hair. I imagined picking pastels out of my box, making strokes of color, bringing this extraordinary hair to life on paper.

Zoe moved her arm slightly. Our wrists touched. My skin rose to meet hers, a movement slow and sensual. Two lovers dancing in the dark.

She was looking at me, her attention fierce, forcing me to complete awareness. "It's Okay," she said. "I'll take care of you."

And she began to do so.

Each time Zoe touched me in a new place or blew on my skin, chills raced across me like water. Unlike with the two boys I'd kissed, there was no hurry, no urgency. It was like music building inside. Each note felt like I would explode. Or die. Maybe I would die.

I did.

And afterward, I lay astonished, an immense body of water without any edges.

Chapter 36

I woke suddenly, my heart thumping.

A noise had registered in my sleeping brain, rhythmic and purposeful, not the random movements of animals.

The moon was high, and from where I lay, looking out through the screened door, wrapped in the blanket against Zoe's body, it illuminated the path to Chad's cabin.

A flashlight was bumping down the path toward us.

I punched Zoe with my elbow. "Someone's coming."

"Mmm."

"Zoe." I dug in. "Wake up!"

"That hurts." She rolled toward me, her hair sticking up, backlit by the moon and lake. I kissed her.

"Someone's on the path."

We could hear a tuneless whistling, punctuated by *shit* and *goddamn tree.*

"Chad," Zoe mouthed. "Get moving, girl." She slipped from the blanket, her body pale against the dark outdoors, quickly blew out the candle. The room slipped into bleached moonlight.

I saw her faint outline bend to pull on jeans.

I felt for my glasses. My underwear.

"Just these," Zoe said. She thrust my jeans into my hands.

I moved like I was underwater, not sure where I was, senses stunned by everything that had happened. We scrambled into our clothes. I was aware of her body, now knowing what everything looked like underneath, but I didn't take time to look.

"Did Chad see the light?"

"He's too wasted." Zoe moved like she was skimming a lake's surface. "Shoes," she commanded. "Over there."

She hefted the pack on her shoulders. "Let's get out of here," she whispered urgently. Chad's mumbling and off-key music was closer.

I lifted the hurricane candle and we slipped out the door. The candle was burning my fingers. I set it at the edge of the porch, away from the steps. With luck, Chad would be too drunk to notice it. I could get it tomorrow.

Chad's flashlight was turning the bend down the main path toward the cabin steps. We ran silently to the far end of the porch, lifted our legs over the rustic railings, and jumped into the bushes. Zoe caught me, crouched, put her arm around me. She smiled, her face inches away.

"Good morning," she whispered, "glory." She kissed me.

I had to smile back. "It's still the middle of the night."

Her whisper tickled my ear. "You're beautiful anytime."

A minute later heavy feet climbed the stairs to the porch. There was a loud stumble and the sound of glass breaking.

"What the hell?" Chad muttered.

"Oops," Zoe whispered. "Another priceless heirloom."

I shook my head. "Aunt Anna's junk."

"Let's hope he goes inside soon. I want to continue where we left off." She nuzzled my neck.

The woods were dark around us, rich and earthy smelling. I shivered, happy and terrified. I didn't think there was more to do than we had already done.

Chad didn't go inside. We heard the creak of one of the

Adirondack porch chairs, the heavy plunk of a body sitting, and whistling began again, still tuneless and meandering. Zoe sighed, settled down on her pack. After a minute we heard the crunch of sticks and leaves under foot.

"Chad?" It was Sarah's voice. "Fuck," she said as she stumbled over a root.

Feet ran up the porch steps.

"Where'd you go?" Sarah's voice wasn't slurred like Chad's. It was angry.

"Nowhere."

"You promised."

"I did not promise you anything." Chad enunciated each word.

Sarah sat in the other Adirondack chair. "We were going to party."

"We did," Chad said. "I did."

"Yeah, and you're totally wasted." Sarah blew out her lips. There was a pause then the scrape of a chair being dragged. Wet sounds like kissing.

"Hold on," Chad said.

"Why?" Sarah's voice, indignant.

"You are rushing me. I don't like being rushed." Chad sounded like the drunk was beginning to wear off.

"I thought you liked it."

"I do."

We heard the rustle of clothing, a zipper being pulled.

Chad groaned.

"Oh, gross," Zoe whispered. "I can't listen to this." She began to get up but her legs buckled. She sat suddenly.

"What the hell was that?" Sarah said.

"Why are you stopping?" Chad mumbled. "I didn't hear anything."

"I did."

Zoe and I stayed perfectly still. I don't even think I was breathing.

"Probably a bear." Chad shifted in his chair. "Or a raccoon."

"That's right," Zoe whispered. I giggled.

"Raccoons don't talk." Sarah's footsteps moved toward our end of the porch. A flashlight shone toward our faces. "God," she said with disgust, "there's someone down here. Come out, you dirtbag, we know you're there."

Zoe raised herself into the wavering flashlight beam.

"Zoe?" Sarah said. "What are you doing down there?"

Zoe hefted her pack. "I lost something when I was visiting Chad the other day."

Sarah glowered at Chad. "What were you looking for?"

"Who is it?" Chad called.

"It's Zoe," Sarah said. I couldn't stand my cramped position anymore and rose too. "And Molly."

We couldn't see Sarah's face behind the flashlight. "Lower that thing. You'll blind someone." Zoe used the same commanding tone as when they were practicing crossovers. Sarah obediently lowered the flashlight. At the same time, the porch light went on and we were all bathed in golden yellow.

"What were you doing down there in the middle of the night?" Sarah frowned at me. "Molly, your shirt is open."

I grabbed my front and frowned back. "So what? I was swimming."

"I lost something," Zoe said again. "Molly was helping me find it." She backed out of the shrubbery and started walking toward the porch steps. I followed, my brain working as furiously as it could after a night with Zoe, waking up suddenly, and hiding in bushes for fifteen minutes listening to my cousin seduce a reluctant neighbor. I knew Sarah wasn't stupid, despite her inane comments most of the time. I figured Chad's stupor was wearing off if he could turn on lights without being asked.

Zoe clomped up the steps and put her backpack on the porch, kicked shards of hurricane lamp out of the way, and sat. I sat too, not as close as I wanted, still watching Sarah watch us.

But she was distracted by the glinting pieces on the porch floor. "Isn't that my mother's?"

"It was," I said. "Until Chad killed it."

"What was it doing over here?" Sarah said. She was looking back and forth, from my face to Zoe's.

"I didn't kill anything," Chad said. He was slumped in the Adirondack chair, eyeing us suspiciously.

"This is all too weird," Sarah said.

"Maybe we should eat something," Zoe said. She was pulling a half-eaten bag of chips out of her pack. "Anybody hungry?"

"I am," Chad said. Zoe handed him the bag. He took a huge handful, stuffed it all in his mouth, began coughing violently. Sarah leaned over and walloped him on the back. A dislodged corn chip flew across the porch floor and landed in a little sodden mass. We all stared at it.

"Well," I said briskly, pushing myself to my feet. "It's way past my bedtime."

"Wait," said Chad. "I have one question."

Zoe and I both stilled.

"Are we skiing tomorrow morning?" He lay his head against the back of the chair like it weighed twenty pounds. "Because I don't think I can drive the boat."

"I'll give you the morning off," Zoe said.

"Excellent," Chad said. He closed his eyes.

"What about me?" Sarah said.

"You take the morning off too," Zoe said.

"'Bye," I said.

We got out of there as fast as we could.

Chapter 37

The moon was clear over the lake, slanting a white path toward Dougall Mountain, bright enough to see each other's faces, although, after all that had happened, I longed for dark.

I sat cross-legged on our dock, listening to the movement of Zoe's feet in the water. Moonlight etched the sneakers and wadded up socks she'd set behind her. I watched her brace herself with her arms and let her head hang. I didn't say anything, just crossed and recrossed my legs four or five times, until I realized how nervous it looked.

"Whew," she finally said.

"Totally." That sounded pretty unintelligent, so I added, "What a night."

"What a night."

This had to be the dumbest conversation we'd ever had.

"Do you think Sarah knew what . . . "

Zoe shrugged. "I just hope she was more obsessed with Chad and mopping him up."

"I've never seen Chad drunk."

"I have," Zoe said. "One time. He said you dumped him." Her head was still hanging toward her knees. "I wouldn't let him drive the next day."

I was smelling her skin and it was driving me nuts. "We haven't ever been out together."

"Didn't you go to a concert in Saranac?"

"That wasn't a date."

"He said he kissed you."

"He said that?" I couldn't believe it. "To you?"

"Yeah, he was bragging about it. Kind of ridiculous, don't you think?"

I could see the outline of her lips in the moonlight. They weren't fashion model lips, plump like bees had stung them, but they suited her. I couldn't stop staring at them, and I think she felt it because the lips began to curve up a tiny bit. It wasn't quite a smile, just a delicate movement, a reminder.

"So," I said.

"So," she said.

"I wondered."

"What?"

The way she was looking at me, even in the pale dark where we were sitting, was something I could feel in every part of my body.

"What do people do afterward?"

Zoe didn't answer. She began to inch one leg, then the other, along the dock until she was sitting as close to me as possible. She scooted even closer, nudging me a bit.

"Are you trying to push me in?"

She shook her head and wrapped both arms around my shoulders, pulling me against her.

"What if Sarah or Chad walks by?" I said, squirming away.

"By people," Zoe said, "do you mean us?"

I ducked out from her arms. "Anybody can see us. It's like daylight out here."

"You care about that now? After everything?"

"Well, yes," I said, annoyed that she thought I was such an innocent. "I haven't got your incredible experience in bed."

Then suddenly, I was jealous. Imagining who else she'd had this conversation with. I got to my feet, brushing off my jeans, skin suddenly hot.

"We weren't exactly in bed," Zoe said mildly. "Cushions on the floor, remember? Way more uncomfortable than any bed I've slept in."

The tension of the evening was accelerating through me. It got so bad for a minute I thought I'd throw up, right in front of her, which would've been a stellar ending to everything, including any interest Zoe might have in me. I focused my breathing on the slope of Dougall Mountain where the black lake met the black trees, where across the lake, a loon called again, and the sound ran through me like cooling water.

"Did you know loons need a long lake so they can land?" I took a deep breath. "They're really heavy birds."

"It's going to be Okay, Molly."

Zoe had gotten up too. Her hug was tight, like she wasn't going to ever let go. I had to lean on her to stay standing.

"How do you know?"

She jiggled me a little. "I just know."

I twisted, but she held tight until I fell against her. I felt my face in her hair, her warm breath. "I just never did this before," I said, my voice muffled. "And you have. Apparently, plenty of times."

"Twice, silly," Zoe said. "I told you that." She kissed me. "You smell so good. I'm a smitten kitten."

"That's a stupid rhyme." I paused. "Only twice?"

Zoe's voice was serious, deeper. "Never like this."

Chapter 38

The next morning I found the last cache of Sammy's. I was helping my mother clean the living room. She was fluffing the sofa cushions but one was lumpier than usual. When I picked it up, there was a small collection of shiny objects underneath.

"Well," my mother said, "my spoons."

Sammy had taken three of them, plus a small metal box my father used for scraps of scratch paper. There was also a ball of gum wrappers. The light glinted off the gathering. My brother was out on the porch, setting up his stuffed animals along the rustic railing so they could watch my father paint in the clearing.

"He borrows things," I told my mother. "He just likes them because they shine in the light." I expected another lecture about stealing, but she was smiling. I watched her place the cushion carefully back over the gathering of shine.

"It'll be our secret," my mother said. She picked up her broom and went toward the porch, toward her son.

When the room was empty I called Zoe. She was getting

ready for waterskiing practice. When I asked her how she was able to ski after such a night, she told me the competition at Daggett Lake was only weeks away.

So was my family's last day at Cloud Lake, I thought. The end of summer and Zoe's possible departure for Los Angeles. My birthday.

I quickly changed the subject. "Did you even sleep at all?"

"An hour," she said. "Maybe. How about you?"

"Same." Outside the window, I could see big thunderheads massing in the west. Whiteface Mountain would be invisible soon. "It's getting stormy."

"I noticed," she said. "But I've got to work out those new bindings. They're still putting my feet to sleep."

It was hard to focus on what we were talking about. I could only feel my skin and bones and heart hurting.

"Can I come watch?" I asked.

"If you want. But I have to warn you, Phil's driving." Zoe sighed. I knew Phil was more trouble than he was worth. And he was drinking a lot more, from stress, Zoe said. "He's been in a pretty mean mood."

"Chad can't do it?"

"I tried calling him. No answer."

"Oh, yeah, I bet he's still sleeping."

In the background, a deep male voice let out a stream of curses. "Time to go," Zoe said. "My ride's waiting." The voice got louder. At the same time, from our porch came an almost answering scream, Sammy's voice saying, "Nonono," and my mother soothing him.

I was suddenly, irrationally, scared.

"Hey, Zoe?"

"Huh?"

"Can you skip practice today?" My words came out fast, tumbling in urgency. "You didn't get hardly any sleep, you know. And it's really going to blow up bad out there, later. You can look in the newspaper if you don't believe me. There may be lightning. You don't want to be out on the lake if there's lightning."

"I won't ski if there's lightning. But I'm too dedicated to stay in just because. Don't you know that by now?" I could hear her smile and her focus through the phone. She was dedicated, single-minded, bulleting toward a championship, not letting anything stop her. I always admired it before, but right now it scared me.

Sammy's voice rose again, another little scream. The sound raced along my skin like sharp fingernails. I was unconsciously twirling the phone cord tighter around my whitening hand. I loosened my grip.

"I'm scared." The words tumbled out before I could stop them. I felt stupid saying it.

"I'm careful," Zoe said. "You know that."

"Yeah."

"Hey, about last night?"

I tried to smile away my fear. "I think I've heard that line before."

"I hope not."

"In a movie, dummy."

"Well, all right." She paused. "I just wanted to say, I'm still swimming."

Her words made my chest relax. Everything would be Okay. We'd figure it out. And as if to confirm it, I heard Sammy's laugh, familiar and high and sweet.

"I haven't even dried off yet," I said. I sent a silly grin toward the suncatcher, spinning uselessly in the window. "I probably never will."

"In case anyone's on your party line," Zoe said, "I'll see you at the usual dock at the usual time. Bring your raincoat, Okay?"

After breakfast, my mother told me they were going into Plattsburgh. "We're getting this shaggy kid a haircut before we can't see his face anymore." Sammy giggled at that. "You want to come?" my mother said.

"I'm going to watch Zoe." I gathered up Sammy's books. We'd been reading over our muffins, spreading butter with our fingers, getting the pages sticky.

My mother looked toward the lake. "It's getting stormy out

there."

"She needs support. Daggett Lake and all."

Sammy was humming, hanging on my mother's leg. "Can we get ice cream?" he sang. "Can we, can we?"

I smiled, letting myself be saturated with this voice I'd missed for weeks. And my mother bent immediately, smiling. "For you? Of course. Shall we ask your daddy if he wants some?"

"Yes!" Sammy shouted.

"Then get your shoes on."

He ran toward the screen door, banged it open, and disappeared.

"Will you be Okay here alone for a couple of hours, Molly?" My mother was smiling at me now. "We'll bring you back some ice cream."

"You'll be back soon?" I said, suddenly afraid again.

She tousled my hair, like I was Sam's age. "I'll be back."

Chapter 39

At the dock the air was thick with approaching storm and a coolness that spoke of winter. The maple nearest the three birches already showed branches of fire-red leaves.

I had put on my bathing suit and my raincoat, and I brought two towels in crazy patterns of red and white, colors easily visible to Zoe skiing across the lake. I spread one flat on the dock and lay down, draping the other towel across my legs. Everything was almost eerily still, the water a silvery gray mirror reflecting dark trees and rocks.

I scanned the lake for movement. Two fishing boats hovered by the driftwood beach. Then I saw the silver gleam of a motorboat and Zoe's white wake behind it. I thought of her hands gripping the tow rope and my stomach flip-flopped.

I had mostly put aside the memory of those hands during the morning's talk with my mother. It was too weird to place them in the same room, to think of Zoe and hear the sweetness of my brother's high voice from the front porch, feel the relief that he hadn't said anything unusual in a few hours, although his sentences were simpler and it felt like he'd lost a year. But as I lay on the dock, letting thoughts surface like fish coming up to breathe, as I finally let myself relax, the night came flooding in.

I had shown her my fat legs. I probably made way too much noise when she was touching me, when it all happened. And what about the fact that now I really was different, like the girls Sarah made fun of, like the girl who hugged the hallway walls at school? Would my locker be graffitied, would I sit alone at lunch? I couldn't even imagine what my parents would say when they found out. But it didn't really matter. I wanted to stand up on our dock and shout to the entire lake, tell everyone on the party line, that Zoe Novato loved Molly Fisher. I'd engrave it on the biggest plaque Lester could hang over the Boat House bar. Even if Zoe went back to Los Angeles, I would know for sure that she loved me.

The sun came out suddenly. I felt the heat of it on my shoulders, like Zoe's massage. Through the dock slats the water was dappled with shafts of green light.

Across the lake, Zoe and Phil were circling. When the boat swung close enough that I could make out the blue bathing suit, I saw her lift one arm. I knew it was for me. I sat up and held my two red-and-white towels toward the sky, as if I were shaking them out. Zoe's arm moved in response. I lay back down.

Right before I fell asleep, I heard the slap of the boat on waves, the silence of a motor stopping. Zoe's voice, shouting something at Phil. But by then, the sun had baked my skin until my eyelids were too heavy to lift. I was almost gone, still listening for Zoe, almost dreaming about Sammy smiling at me. My feet were twitching under the towel, ballet moves I used to know, or running to get to her.

When I woke up, at least an hour had passed. The sun was completely gone. Late afternoon fishing boats were already white specks on the far shore. I listened for the motorboat. All was still, the sky a thick cottony gray.

Squinting into the paleness, I scanned the lake. That's when I saw the flash: a pale strip of light raised in the air, moving slowly from side to side.

"Molly," I heard, far away as wind on a mountain.

I first looked up the hill, thinking the voice came from the cabin, from my mother or Sammy. But there was none of the noise of a family back from getting ice cream cones. I was still alone.

I heard the voice again. "Come get me. Help me."

"Zoe?" I called, as loud as I could. Some birds chattering behind me suddenly quieted.

"Molly, I'm out here!"

The strip of light waved again. My eyes strained. It looked like someone in the middle of the lake, someone on the surface of the water, waving something in the air.

Usually on a summer afternoon, you could hear people—the Andersons laughing next door, playing bridge or bingo. Kids Jet Skiing from the Boat House rentals. But nothing stirred except the birds and the approaching storm. My mind tried to make sense of what I was seeing, hearing. Zoe was in trouble. How could I get to her, get help? Mr. Anderson was in Las Vegas. Chad or Sarah? I thought about the extra minutes if they weren't there. How long could Zoe hang out on top of the water, holding onto a water ski? How long since she fell that last time? Where was the motorboat? Where was Phil?

I picked up my red towel and waved it high in the air. Zoe answered with a wave of the ski, but when I tried to call out to her, to say I would come get her, no matter what, my voice didn't work.

A cold sweat was gathering on my back. My legs turned up the hill to the cabin, and I began to run like I had that morning Sammy almost died.

My dad had only taken the boat out twice all summer, and not once since the accident. The ring of keys was always handy. I pulled them off the hook, the metal familiar and cold, like the shock of lake water against summer skin. The edge of each key felt like it could cut my hand.

I ran back down to the dock and grabbed all the life preservers

I could carry from the storage bin. I threw them into the stern of the boat. Five orange jackets, puffy with Styrofoam, bright candy against gray metal. Buoyant enough to keep anyone afloat.

Stepping onto the boat, I had to hold my breath. The lake was the stillness before a storm in the Adirondacks, waiting and dangerous. Sourness flooded the back of my mouth and my throat was so tight I could hardly swallow it down.

I heard Zoe again. I inserted the key.

It had been weeks since anyone started the engine. For a few seconds, it whined and gasped. A thin gray exhale came from the back of the boat.

"No," I shouted, "not now." Not when I'd finally gotten up the courage to do this impossible thing. If Zoe drowned out there, I wouldn't be able to live. We were going to be together.

I pressed hard on the choke and turned the key again.

The motorboat rattled to life.

I inhaled deeply to the count of ten, trying to get enough air, calculating distance to the opposite shore, a straight line this time. Suddenly certainty flooded me and with it came the image of Sammy, laughing and safe.

My hands knew just how much to pull back on the throttle. How to gracefully turn the cracked plastic wheel, hot from the sun. How to arc clear of shore.

I gunned it.

Chapter 40

Cloud Lake was small from the wheel of a fast-moving boat, only three-fourths of a mile to the tree-lined side, less to where Zoe floated. Her legs were draped over the neon-pink slalom ski. She was sculling with her hands.

"Thank God." She struggled to raise herself. "I can't feel anything. My legs."

"Hang on," I said. "I'll get you in the boat."

"I know you will."

The trust in her voice sang in my belly. I began to circle Zoe with the Chris Craft, trying for the best angle to lift her out of the water.

I dropped over the stern into the lake, keeping my head above water, my glasses on, keeping myself breathing regularly even as the shock of cold hit my chest. "You'll have to help me."

"Okay." Zoe reached for my hands, her teeth chattering.

"I can't believe Phil left you out here." I was out of breath, struggling with the life jackets.

"He was drunk." Tears ran down Zoe's cheeks, mingling

with the sheen of lake water. "I said I wanted to swim home. He actually believed me." She was shivering like crazy. "I'm so cold."

"We'll get you warm." I threaded her arms through one of the life jackets, held another under her head. Like Sammy, she weighed next to nothing. The water was like glass, the boat motionless. I could drag her to the stern without even losing breath.

Once Zoe's fingers were on the bottom rung, I heaved myself up the ladder and pulled her into the boat. We collapsed into the bottom of the Chris Craft. Zoe closed her eyes and her shoulders began to shake. I wrapped her tightly in both the towels, held her as close as I could.

We both lay there for a while, breathing hard. She snaked out one hand from the cocoon of towels and I took it, grasping the thin elegant fingers like they were my life preserver. Against the side of the boat, the slalom ski floated upside down like a marker.

We got back to the dock before anyone got home but not before Phil came by, in the boat, looking for Zoe. I recognized him immediately. He was dressed in an orange hunting vest and raggedy jeans. He was obviously still wasted.

"Get off the lake," I shouted over the wind, pulling my jacket around Zoe. "It's dangerous."

"Zoe, get back in this boat," he said, swaying a little, ignoring me. "We're going home."

I put my arms around her, not caring if he saw me. The wind died for a minute, and the boat's engine was loud in our ears. "She's been hurt," I said to Phil. "I'm taking her up to our cabin and my mother's going to take care of her." I tugged on Zoe's arm. She was shivering again, not from cold this time.

"What's wrong, Zoe? Where are you hurt?" Phil's eyes swung between us.

"Everywhere, you jerk. You left me in the lake. What did you expect?" She started coughing.

"You told me to leave you." He looked bewildered, pushing up his black feed cap to get a better look at her. "You said you were going to swim back. You said it wasn't that far."

Zoe was breathing heavy, and her face was red. Her words came out clipped. "How many parents would leave their kids in the middle of the lake, Phil. Just think about it."

"We need to get her warm and dry." I was turning Zoe up the hill as I spoke. "My mother will call you when she's better. She may stay with us for a few days." I had no idea if my mother would agree to this. Phil was silent. "My mother is good with emergencies," I added. "She's a airplane pilot." I looked back at him, willing him to believe me, to leave her alone.

"Well, Okay." Phil rubbed his hands on the steering wheel, then bent toward the throttle. "I don't have your phone number."

"She'll call you," I said.

Zoe muttered something.

"Better get off the lake," I said. "It's no place to be in a storm."

We didn't look back, just heard the pulse of the engine as the boat began moving away from the dock.

"Maybe he'll get struck by lightning." Zoe was leaning on my arm, picking her way along the path. Tears were running down her cheeks. She stumbled every few steps.

I held on tighter. "Are you Okay?"

She was walking like she couldn't feel if her feet were even on the ground. "Those idiot bindings."

"We'll take care of your feet too."

Above us, a car crunched on the gravel drive. I heard doors slam, my brother's voice, my mother's answering laugh. "My mom really is good with this stuff," I said. "She had all this training when she got her license." Zoe slipped a little and I pulled her upright. "It's only a little farther. You can make it."

"Are you going to tell her?" Zoe said.

"About us?"

"That you drove the boat."

I shook my head. "Probably not."

"About us, then."

I thought of the talk last Sunday, my mother's hands on my face. "Things are pretty good right now. I don't know if they could take another shock from me."

We were approaching the porch steps. In the misty rain, the

yellow bug light glowed, the cedars' pungent smell all around us. I could hear my brother running down the path from the parking area, my parents following more slowly. I led Zoe up onto the porch and sat us both on the swing.

Sammy arrived first, his little feet pounding up the steps, his yellow slicker flapping. "I had two ice cream cones!" he said. "Two!" He flung himself at me, and I gave him a big squeeze.

My brother, I mouthed to Zoe. She nodded.

"What kind, Sammy Sam?" I said.

"Chocolate." His voice was muffled. "Pineapple."

"They make pineapple ice cream?" Zoe said.

"Strawberry," Sammy said. "Pineapple is only juice." He lifted his head and stared at Zoe. "Your hair's all wet."

"It's raining," I said.

"I was waterskiing," Zoe said.

"She's a champion water-skier," I said. "Her name's Zoe."

Sammy seemed as fascinated by Zoe as I was. "Are you Molly's friend?"

"Most definitely."

"I'm Sam Fisher."

Zoe held out her hand. "Glad to know you. Wanna shake?"

Sammy grabbed her hand and pumped it once or twice.

"Your sister talks about you a lot," Zoe said. "You're her favorite brother."

Sammy wrapped his arms around my waist and burrowed in my lap. I felt his hum like a vibration, a purr against my legs. "I'm her only brother."

I put my hand on his head and held it there, feeling the pulse of his little body, my heart amazed and happy.

My parents were coming up the steps, my mother's hair bright and sparkling with rain.

"Miss Molly," my father said, "the girl who missed some awesome ice cream."

"This is my friend Zoe," I said.

"You're the water-skier," my mother said. "Sarah will never be the same. Our family owes you a big debt. She thinks you walk on water."

"She water skis," Sammy said. "And she's Molly's friend."

My father was studying Zoe. "Where have you competed?" he asked. "Placid?"

"How do you know about that stuff?" I asked.

"Your dad was a pretty good skier in his day," my mother said.

I laid my hand on Sammy's head again. It was soft as down. He didn't back away or frown at my touch, just smiled up at me. "Well, Zoe's been in the water a bit too long today. She needs to get warmed up. If that's Okay."

"Of course it's Okay," my mother said. "Shower, food, dry clothes." She peered at us. "Looks like you both could use those."

"Isn't there another competition in a few weeks?" my father asked. "Daggett Lake?"

Zoe nodded.

"Slalom, isn't it? Are you competing?"

She was pushing herself to her feet, wiggling her toes. She put weight on both legs, and they held. "Looks like I'll be there," she said, smiling up at my father. "Despite everything."

When Zoe was in the shower, letting steam wash away the afternoon, I brought her towels. She poked her head out and I kissed her as silently as I could, letting the pounding water insulate us for a moment. Then I shut the door behind me.

My mother was making cocoa in the kitchen. "Have I met your friend before?" she asked. She set five mugs on the table and a small bag of marshmallows. I fingered one, wadding it into a powdery ball.

"She's at the Boat House a lot."

"Is Sarah still skiing with her?"

"I don't think so."

"Zoe seems very nice," my mother said. The cocoa gulped on the stove and she stirred it.

"She may need a place to stay until the competition."

"I thought you said she was renting down at Lester's. With her father. What's his name?"

"Phil Novato," I said. Agent to lesser-known Hollywood stars. "He's going back to Los Angeles."

"I guess Zoe could stay with us." She looked a little worried. "Does she know about Sammy?"

"Sammy likes her."

"She'd have to share with you, Molly. Good thing we kept the big bed out there on your porch."

The saucepan made another slurping sound and my mother said, "Cocoa's ready."

We heard the shower stop, the slide of shower curtain rings on the wooden rail my father had made, a low humming from Zoe toweling herself off. Fragrant chocolate steam filled the kitchen and in it I could see every detail of her at that moment, even though my eyes were watching my mother's hands lift the saucepan and carefully divide the cocoa between five mugs. I dropped three marshmallows into each, set the mugs on our round yellow tray, and carried them into the main room.

Zoe came out, her hair wrapped in a big towel, wearing the jeans and sweatshirt I'd lent her. The jeans bagged at the seat. "They almost fit," she said, turning. "Don't they?"

I lowered my voice a little. "You look great," I said.

"Molly Tamale." She was looking at me like I was something hot. I flushed. Her lips moved upward at the corners. They were all pink and pearly from the hot water. She noticed me watching, and her smile got bigger like she wanted to throw me down on the couch right in our living room and kiss me until I was swooning again.

"Did you want some cocoa?" I said.

"Not as much as you." The way she said this, my mother or father wouldn't have noticed anything. I knew what she meant. My face got even redder.

"You're not a very careful person," I said. "Are you."

"You handle that for both of us." Zoe stretched high and the towel fell off her hair, almost into the fire. I swung myself toward her and grabbed it. "Thanks," she said, not smiling anymore. "I'm glad, about you being careful."

Sammy came rushing in from the porch, followed by my father. The phone rang and my mother answered it.

"It's Sarah for you," she called.

"Tell her I'm busy," I said.

"Hey! Cocoa puffs!" Sammy said, pointing to the mugs.

"Just cocoa," I said. "Want some?"

He nodded. I handed him the mug with the dancing bears. "It's really hot, so be careful."

I flushed when I said it. I could feel Zoe smiling at me again.

Chapter 41

Zoe was staying at our house and sleeping in my bed. For three weeks, with her father's Okay, until the competition.

I couldn't believe my luck.

I tried to be first to wake in the morning, just to see the light touch her face. Even though she was the quietest sleeper, Sammy's bed had been moved into the main room near the fire. So except for my parents next door, we were private.

I loved to watch Zoe's mouth move when she dreamed, how she drooled a little on the pillow, how her parted lips received air then let it go soundlessly. We only kissed when everyone was away from the cabin, and as far as my family knew, Zoe and I were just friends who whispered and giggled as we fell asleep.

I watched my father especially closely during this time. Maybe even he didn't suspect because Zoe got along so well with everyone. She was extra polite, talking waterskiing shop with my dad at dinner, complimenting my mother on every herb in the soup. My parents were also preoccupied with a growing truce that made them more and more relaxed with each other.

Sammy coming home was making things better, not worse, as I had feared.

The only real storm was Zoe's daily phone calls with Phil. She would shout at him and hang up, crying. She tried not to do this in front of my parents or Sammy, but once the phone rang when they were out on the porch. We heard their conversation suddenly quiet.

My mother came in, pushing open the screen door almost silently, and stood there, waiting.

"He's such a jerk," Zoe said, swiping at her face. "Sorry."

My mother put an arm around Zoe, led her to the couch. I watched them snuggle, feeling jealous, and my mother raised her head and caught me with her eyes, gestured for me to come join them. I sat on her other side and my mother held one of us in each arm.

"Adults can be total jerks." She gestured again and I grabbed the box of tissues from the end table. Zoe blew her nose loudly.

"He's not that bad." Her voice was muffled. "Except when he's stressed. The studio wants him to go to Japan. He wants me to stay with my grandmother."

I held my breath.

"Where does she live?" my mother asked.

"This tiny apartment in Plattsburgh. She doesn't have room for me. And we don't get along very well."

"How long will your father be gone?"

Zoe shrugged. "Movies can take a whole year. Especially with bad acting."

"What about your mother? Couldn't you stay with her?"

I wanted to interrupt now, tell my mom to stop asking questions, but Zoe answered. "She travels a lot. She's an artist." Zoe sniffled a little. "Summer's her busiest time. We haven't been able to reach her. I think she's in Australia now."

At least Australia was an English-speaking country, I thought. You could talk on the phone. But Zoe never mentioned phone calls with her mother. And now I heard that same wistfulness in her voice that I'd noticed on the climb that day. "You could stay with us," I said. "Just for the school year, until your mom gets back." I pitched my voice low, not too high and hopeful.

My mother looked at me, then at Zoe. "Well."

"It'd be easy," I rushed on. "You could ride the bus with me."

"Would your father go for that?" my mother asked.

"Phil would kiss you for it," Zoe said slowly. She made a little grimace at the thought, blew her nose again. Then she smiled at me so big, I thought I'd burst. "It would solve a lot of problems."

It sounded like a promise. Something I could count on. Amazement surged in my chest. Things didn't usually turn out this well in my life.

"I'll have to ask Molly's dad," my mother said. "We'll talk it over. You'd need to ask your mother too."

"She'd say yes, I know it. But I could call her studio to be sure. Someone would know how to get ahold of her." Zoe smiled a little, and I wondered if her artist mother was anything like my artist father. "I'm sure she'd say yes," she said again, smiling even bigger at me.

I slowly let my breath out. Zoe in my bed for weeks. Months. Going to school with me every day. With all that had happened, it was almost too much to think about.

Even though the accident was now family history, its effects lingered, visible to me every day in my brother's halting healing, in how his brain worked now. My immediate surges of guilt had been mostly replaced by gladness at having him home. I knew he and I would talk. But I wasn't afraid anymore that he had stopped loving me. In fact, because of Zoe, I felt cracked open inside, able to love Sammy even deeper.

We took him to Plattsburgh on August tenth for tests. They weren't the kind of tests where you got an A and a teacher's neat cursive *Good work!* The doctors were monitoring Sammy's rehabilitation. They wanted to see if the parts of his brain that had gone on vacation were back. From the Web sites on comas, I knew it was routine. Monitoring the patient's progress, they called it. How the brain was recovering from the TBI. Out of Sammy's hearing, we all used that term now—*TBI* meant "traumatic brain injury."

"Tell me all the animals you can think of when I say go." The therapist nodded toward her watch, her neat cap of blond hair catching the fluorescents.

Sammy said *cat, dog, raccoon, giraffe,* looked at me, added *lion, bear.* I smiled. The therapist pointed to pictures in a book, Sammy shrugged thin shoulders under his red T-shirt, named them. She gave him a box, told him to put something inside. Remove it. *If this is in, what's that called?* "Out," he said.

We all stopped for ice cream on the way home, celebrating that Sammy hadn't called the bathroom a bathtub since that first day. We didn't tell the therapist that breakfast cereals were hard to remember. Or simple words like *fireplace.* They'd find out soon enough.

Sammy smiled and cried and got mad, and he lay under the cabin humming little songs again. The words came out funny, but the tunes were the same as before the accident. I heard him everywhere.

My father began cleaning the motorboat. Sammy and I watched. Sammy yelled, "Hi, ducks," and laughed as they scattered from the float. But he didn't remember the accident. "When are you going to take me out in the boat, Molly?" he said over and over. "You promised for my birthday, didn't you?" The details of the accident and the jackknife that had changed all our lives on June fifteenth had slowly erased themselves.

I hugged him, told him soon. This adorable stranger in our house was sure he lived here. He was someone I could almost recognize.

One afternoon, when Sam and I were sitting on his boulder watching Zoe practice, he suddenly leaned against me.

"I keep dreaming of winter, Meemee. Snowshoes in the woods." He turned and looked into my face. "Just us. And this red bird on a branch. Did that happen, ever?"

"Probably." I paused. "Do you remember your birthday?"

Sam shook his head. His hair moved soft against my bare arm.

"I was silly," I said, "on your birthday. I'm sorry. I did

something really stupid. But I was just trying to give you the very best birthday present. You believe me, don't you?"

Sammy nodded, the silky hair massaging my skin. "You wouldn't do anything stupid, Meemee. Not on purpose."

"Well, it wasn't on purpose. But I need to say I'm sorry anyway."

"It's Okay," my baby brother said. "Hey, do you think we could go snowshoeing in the woods when the snow comes?"

"It'll be months before that."

"But we'll all be here together. When the snow comes."

"Maybe Dad will take us." I put an arm around his shoulders, pulling him closer. His little body was so thin, but we'd get him healthy again.

"I want to go with just you and me," said Sam. He rubbed his ear, looked up at me. "It would be the very best present."

Chapter 42

With all the excitement of Sammy's homecoming and Zoe in my bed, I hadn't talked much with my father. I hadn't put the new knife in his desk drawer. In the evenings after dinner, I would look up sometimes and catch him studying me. As if he were trying to work an uncompleted puzzle. As if he knew I still held a piece he was missing, a secret just out of reach.

So I wasn't surprised one morning when I heard footsteps on the path and saw him walking toward me from his studio, his face determined.

It was about ten o'clock, and the sun was already high and hot. Zoe was long since on the lake, and my mother and Sammy had driven the truck into town for groceries.

"Molly," my father said. "Do you have a minute?"

He was wearing a red baseball cap. I set my book aside, a finger in the pages, watching him take it off. He stood beside my chair, tall and unsmiling.

"Your mother said you had something to tell me. Something important."

My father's clouds and brightness were familiar to me. I'd learned to position myself to his mood. Today all I wanted was peace, rest from another active night with Zoe. I could just imagine what he would say when I showed him the knife. I probably would never get the entire story out, much less hear him apologize for his part in it.

So I shrugged. "It's nothing."

"That's not what your mother said."

"You'll just get mad at me. Like you always do. Even when something's not entirely"—and I stressed the word—"my fault."

My father looked out at the lake and sighed. He sank into the Adirondack chair next to my wicker one.

"Am I really that scary?"

I didn't know what to say. I thought of my father chopping wood, his fierceness, the intensity with which he absorbed a subject and translated it to canvas. I'd woken up that morning, wanting to paint too. Lying in bed, I imagined standing in front of my easel, my father joining me, painting side by side in the clearing as silently and companionably as we used to. Despite the growing peace, despite his newly gentle sketches of Sam, it would never happen.

I swallowed thickly. "It's just hard to tell you things. You get so upset."

"I'll try to stay calm."

"Okay. How about this? Sam's accident wasn't all my fault. It happened because of Willie's jackknife."

My father started like someone had knocked into him. He took off his glasses, wiped his forehead with his palm.

"Have you looked for it lately?" I continued.

"It's in the drawer in my desk."

"Actually, it's not."

Reactions played across his face: confusion, anger, sadness. "How could you kids take it again? After everything we've been through?"

I launched to my feet. My book fell to the floor and thwacked the porch boards. My father glared at it.

"How could you say that?" I screamed at him. "You never

cared about anything I've been through this summer." I didn't try to stop the tears that flooded in after the words, even though I'd never cried in front of my father.

He reached into his pocket and handed me his handkerchief. I sank back into the chair and blew my nose loudly.

"You don't ever want to hear my side of the story," I said, "just hold on to your own. So you can stay mad forever." I let myself sob, holding the handkerchief to my face, looking out at him through its veil.

"I'm listening now," he said quietly.

The jackknife in my pocket felt small and hard, a story folded up and waiting. After a few minutes, I pulled a small table between his big green Adirondack chair and my white wicker one. I felt in my pocket and started to pull out the rose quartz but reached further.   Soon the jackknife lay on the table between us, blade folded in.

He looked up at me, peered at the knife. "What's this?"

"It's not Willie's."

"I can see that."

"Willie's is in the lake."

My father leaned back against the chair's ribbed backrest. He was wearing a light gray T-shirt and it contrasted with the dark green chair in a nice way that made me feel a tiny bit calmer, a tiny bit friendlier toward him.

"Do you want to hear why?"

"You said Sammy had it the day of the accident."

"Yes, he did."

I began my story. When I was finished, my father took his glasses off and wiped them slowly, staring at the jackknife, memories playing across his face.

Watching him, a memory of my own came.

I was eight, and we were summering here at Cloud Lake for the first time. He had taken me down to the lake one morning before anyone was up. It was our last day at the cabin that year and I wore a yellow slicker against a drizzle that had started while we were sleeping. My father's glasses misted with rain. He kept taking them off to wipe clean on his shirt, the same way he was wiping them now.

The dock had been taken out the day before and it lay by the rocks, stacked in long slabs. We crouched near the lake, not talking. Eventually I looked up at my father and saw wet rivulets on his cheeks.

"Daddy?" I said.

He pointed. In the water, bright against the gray stillness, floated a fallen sheaf of crimson maple leaves.

My father's shoulders were twitching like they hurt. His face, so like mine, reflecting in the same still water, was stunned. Years later, I realized his pain came from what he saw, how he knew he could never be adequate to it. Beauty pierced my father's heart and made him unfit for the world. In this way, we were both the same and different.

Now he put a hand to his eyes and lowered his head. His shoulders shook violently, once. Then he pulled himself up, looking at me, his glasses partly fogged again.

"It was the best gift I could think of," he said. "He just wouldn't let up. I thought, what's the harm?" His eyes were helpless with regret.

"I know." I reached out and put a hand on his arm, and to my surprise, he covered it with his own hand. The warmth of his palm on the skin of my hand transmitted terrible hurt, but it was something he was letting me share. We sat in silence a bit longer. I knew there was more to say but I was listening to the wind in the cedars now, letting it right my world. I studied the clearing, empty, my card table and still life put away, and saw a late-season hummingbird dash toward the feeder. Soon they would all be gone.

My father saw it too and stirred. "Where'd the other knife come from?" he asked.

"Anna found it in Willsboro."

Small lettering was etched on the jackknife handle. My father read it, USMC, then looked out at the trees. "Willie's brother was in the Marines too. We were all in basic together. They shipped out before we did. I think he lived around here. Maybe I should find him." He looked up at me. "What do you think?"

I could count on one hand the number of times my father asked my thoughts, wanted my advice. I started to rush forward to meet him, to automatically obey the sound of his voice. Instead, I imagined Zoe, how she lived completely in herself, sure of the wind and the water and just how much to lean into the pull of the tow rope that escorted her across the surface of a lake. I let silence fill the space between us, let the lake and the midday birds and the wind chime help me find myself without him.

"Well," he said finally, gathering himself up. "I'll go get some steel wool and clean the blade a little." He held the knife, studying it. I knew he was sorry Willie's knife was gone, lost forever in the bottom of the lake. But I also noticed something had changed in my father's face as he held this newer knife. After a minute, he folded his fingers and the knife disappeared into his big hand like those memories never existed.

"I owe you some money."

He looked up.

"I borrowed it from your studio. When Sammy was in the hospital."

His face was neutral, as if he were calculating my words against what had just happened between us.

As I watched a slow acceptance come into his eyes, I said, "I'll pay it back. I promise."

"I know." He put on his red baseball cap. I stood too. We stayed there for a few seconds.

When my father reached out and gathered me into his arms, I leaned into him in a new way, still myself, but welcoming his embrace too. He was tall enough for my head to tuck under his chin. I laid my cheek against his collarbone and his gray T-shirt, laundered so many times, smelling of pastel dust and Adirondack wood smoke and the cedar-filled wilderness—those things I loved as he did.

My father held me a long time and I didn't resist. Finally he squeezed me hard and let me go.

As he was walking into the cabin, before he let the screen door slap behind him, he turned.

"You have a birthday this week, don't you?"

"Sweet sixteen," I said.

"Want to go to that place in Placid you like? Nicola's?"

"I'd rather go to Daggett Lake."

"The waterskiing competition?"

"Zoe's doing the slalom race."

"We could all go," my father said. "I'd like to see it again." I couldn't remember when I'd seen his face so smooth and even. He laughed a little. "I might even recognize some of the skiers. The old ones."

"Sarah will want to come," I said. "Chad. Anna. You and mom. And Sammy."

"The gang's all here."

My father nodded, his face serious and thankful.

Chapter 43

Daggett Lake was near Warrensburg, south of Cloud Lake. It was a long three hours. I sat in the backseat of the station wagon, wedged between Sarah and my mother who held Sammy on her lap. Sarah shifted and jabbed me with her elbow, muttering in my ear about what Chad did last night and where she was going with Chad tomorrow.

Anna drove like a bat out of hell, my dad next to her, unperturbed, reading maps and calling out directions.

My mother told Sammy a story about a family of rabbits living under the cabin. As soon as she finished, he wanted to hear it again.

Because of all the practice and focus on the competition, Zoe and I hadn't talked about our plans. Her almost-promise to stay, go to high school with me. I'd noticed a gradual distance, Zoe changing the subject the few times I'd brought it up, but generally I was too blissed out to notice.

Today, she drove with her father, the same drunken idiot who'd left her in the middle of the lake to swim home when she couldn't even feel her feet. I listened to Sarah prattle on about Chad, and I was grateful that Chad was with them. If Phil decided to be mean, Chad could protect Zoe.

After an hour, Sarah plugged into her iPod and was quiet. My mother sang to Sammy and he slouched into sleep against my shoulder, his hair sifting gently in the breeze from the open window. Soon it was only the hum of the tires and the shifting sun in and out of the car windows, the occasional lift and sigh of my brother's head. I tried to ignore the tinny whine of Sarah's country and western tunes and concentrate on what lay ahead.

There weren't too many cars at Daggett Lake when we pulled up. We all climbed out, stiff and cranky, into the wooded parking lot of the campground. Before us wound a trail down through the campsites toward the lake. I lifted the picnic basket and my birthday cake out of the trunk.

The sky was scudded with gray and white, broken by sudden brilliant patches of blue that were covered again in minutes. When a breeze came through, the white pines shook drops of rain on our shoulders. My mother looked up worriedly. "Is there a picnic shelter?"

"There's one at the lake," my father said. He shook out his long legs.

Anna's red hair frizzed even more as she got out of the car. She plunked her bags down next to the fender, like she didn't want to go any farther, but Sammy was already galloping toward the lake, his arms outstretched like wings. "Sam and I will get us a table," my mother said, running after him.

I watched my brother's glee, feeling immensely happy for a moment. Then I remembered Zoe and started scanning the parking lot for Phil's white SUV. It was pulling up near a group of boat trailers. Zoe got out slowly, then Chad. He was wearing a yellow Windbreaker that made him look very tan. Zoe was looking around, eyes shaded by one bare arm.

When she saw me, she waved. "Molly!"

Phil turned to look, gave a small lift of hand.

"Go on," Anna said. She took the picnic basket and smiled in a way that made me wonder if she suspected Zoe and I were in love.

I set the cake on the hood of the station wagon. "Save me a piece," I said.

Chad was pulling skis out of the trunk as I ran up. He smiled at me. I stepped past him toward Zoe.

"Hey," I said, pulling her away from the car.

"Hey yourself."

"How are you doing? Are you psyched?"

"Mildly." She nodded. "Or slightly more."

"You're so cool." I reached over and tickled her ribs, and she bent, laughing.

"Stop, you clown. I have to get ready. Chad!"

Chad came over slowly, looking at us.

"Can you help me get all this stuff down to the lake? Molly is useless." She was still grinning like a fool at me. I was sure Chad could see exactly what was going on. Somehow I didn't care.

But he just said, "Sure," and hefted two of her skis.

"I can help too," I said. "For a few minutes. Then I've got to get back to my birthday party."

"Does the cake look good?"

"My mother won't let me see it yet." I lifted another slalom ski out of the back of the SUV. This one had two sleek boots attached. "Do you really need all these?"

"I might. If those bindings don't work." She turned to me, a grimace on her face. "They make you wear stupid life jackets when you ski. Rules of the competition."

Phil was back in the SUV, playing with the radio. Bursts of disconnected sound came toward us through the open back hatch. They blended with the gathering noises from people arriving for the competition. Women and men were unloading ski equipment and picnic baskets and umbrellas.

"I think life jackets are a good idea," I said. "Chad, are you helping the whole time or can you join us for some of my birthday cake?"

"I guess."

"Sarah will probably feed it to you," Zoe grinned.

Chad blew out a mouthful of air, stuck his free hand in his jeans pocket. "You guys have it better."

"Huh?" I said.

"It's Okay," he said and walked toward the lake.

"I thought guys were clueless," Zoe said.

I was following Chad's progress down the trail, the yellow Windbreaker disappearing into the dark pines. "He doesn't seem to mind," I said. "Do you think he'll tell Sarah? It'll be all over school if he does that."

Eventually, I knew I'd tell Anna, my parents, even Sarah. But I wanted to do it in my own timing. I was just sixteen; I was still a child in my parents' eyes, even though I knew I wasn't at all anymore, not after what happened with Zoe in the cabin.

We both stood, watching Chad adjust the skis as he walked, watching Sarah reach him, reach out, Chad turn away.

"I don't think he will tell Sarah," Zoe said thoughtfully. "He likes us. He really likes you."

Phil got out of the car, beer can resting on a brass belt buckle below the slight bulge of his belly. His jeans were black and tight over short leather boots, and his graying hair slicked back under the black feed cap. I saw nothing of Zoe in his face except the gray eyes. "I'm going to go scout. You ladies got things covered here?"

"We always do," Zoe said.

"You make us proud out there, tiger." He saluted us with the beer can and ambled off.

"Is he already drunk?" I asked, watching his weaving steps past a family arguing on the trail.

"He's always like that," Zoe said. "In a way, it's easier. Everyone will totally get it when I don't go back to L.A."

I watched Zoe turn away from me, her attention caught by some flash of light across the parking lot, and the blank wall of her back suddenly terrified me. As she bent to pull out a shortie wet suit in bright lime, a white envelope floated out of the bag, sliding to the ground. The return address read New York, NY.

"You have to wear one of those? It's not that cold."

"Everyone does in competition." She held the wet suit up to

her chest. "Like the color? I picked it out myself."

"It's very nice." I cleared my throat. "Hey, Zoe, can I ask you something?"

"Sure."

"I thought you were staying with us, for a while at least. Remember we talked about it? My parents said yes. I even figured out how we could take the school bus together."

"I've been meaning to talk to you about that. I got this letter yesterday." She pawed through the bags on the ground. "Damn, I know I packed it."

I toed the envelope. "Is this it?"

She bent quickly to pick it up.

"Who's it from?" I asked.

"My mother. Can you believe it?" She smiled big, like I'd be glad too. But something was rising in my throat, pushing it shut. All I could do was nod.

"Yeah, after all this time, she writes and asks me to come stay with her. For the entire year, go to the arts high school in the city."

I'd hardly noticed that it was really starting to rain. Families in brightly colored slickers were opening umbrellas as they exited cars, holding them over food and kids, moving fast toward the picnic shelter. I saw Chad carrying a bag for my mother. When I didn't answer, Zoe began clattering skis.

I put one hand on her arm to stop her movement.

"I thought your mom was an artist," I said carefully. "I thought she was traveling all the time." I almost said, *I thought she didn't love you*, but I bit back the words.

Zoe was watching Chad and my family, my mother and Sammy. Everyone was laughing, not loud enough that we could hear, but we could see their smiles.

"She's going to have surgery," she said. "She needs me to help her."

When Zoe finally looked at me, her shoulders slumped a little. I was fighting tears. She leaned over to pull me close but I pushed her away, violently.

"I thought I could count on you," I shouted.

"You can."

"Apparently not."

"I have to do this, Molly." Her voice pleaded with me to understand. Her thin shoulder blades stood out like wings against the blue bathing suit straps. "I don't even know her. She's never wanted me, needed me before. And now she does. I probably wouldn't have said yes before. But this summer, well, a lot changed. I've changed. Because of you."

Rain was streaking her face and my arms and head, but I didn't care. "I don't get it," I said stubbornly. "If you really," I couldn't say *love*, "if I really mattered, why would you leave me?"

She sighed, wiped her face with the back of her arm. Her hair was wilder than ever from the misty rain, a silky red halo around her head and neck that stood out fiercely against the green and brown of the woods.

"I'm not really leaving you. I'm just going to take care of my mom. For a little while. I have to. She needs me. You get that, don't you?"

Yes, I got that. My brother needed me. My parents, surprisingly, needed me too. Did anyone need Zoe, before this? Maybe just me.

"New York City's not that far," she said gently.

My skin hurt, like I had a fever. She put a palm on my arm, but I didn't jerk it away.

"You could come visit. Every weekend even. It's only five hours by car."

"I don't have a car."

"Six on the Trailways bus, then."

The loudspeaker from the lake blared, announcing that the competition was starting in just ten minutes, and I suddenly saw Zoe's hands on a tow rope, then reaching past me toward the person Zoe needed most right now.

"Does anyone else know?"

"Anna," Zoe said. "I told her yesterday." At my look, she added, "It was because of your birthday. I wanted to recommend a present."

I stared at her hand on my arm, the white webs between each

tanned finger, felt the light massage of them pressing deep into my bones. "I could meet you at Port Authority," she said, her fingers persuading. "You could stay in my room. My mother would be fine with us."

"How do you know? You haven't seen her in years."

Zoe flinched a little. "She hasn't changed. She fell in love with a woman once. That's why she left my dad. And why I had to live with him. It was the dark ages; they'd never allow it now."

We heard Phil's loud laugh from down the trail, and Zoe grimaced. "You'd like my mom's paintings." I watched her say these words, the light in her face when she said them, watched her bend and lift a pack. "New York City has great museums and shows. Fun stuff."

This isn't fun at all! I wanted to shout. *It's my birthday!* But all I said was, "I know." Adirondackers weren't total dweebs. Our class had taken two trips to Manhattan last year.

The loud speaker crackled and screeched again, reminding us why we were standing here. Zoe hoisted another pack. "I've got to get ready." She paused, searching my face. "Will you come watch me win?"

I nodded. My eyes were filling again, but I pretended it was just the rain.

Chapter 44

Zoe did win. For an hour she sped back and forth across the small watercourse, zig-zagging around the bobbing markers, a plume of white flying behind her. My family huddled under the picnic shelter when it began to pour, but I stood on the grass by the lake, my Windbreaker hood dripping beads of water on my nose. I wasn't the only one watching Zoe. Big guys with beer bellies stared at her and made stupid jokes, sleek water-skiers in wet suits whistled as she raced the lake. A teenager with intent eyes cursed each time she rounded the last buoy.

Zoe beat them all, placing first in every slalom course in her class.

She was grinning when she came up to us, red hair plastered to her head, wrapped in a beach towel, holding out a pile of dinky ribbons. I hugged her, proud, even though she was pretty wet, and she draped the ribbons on my head, laughing. I kept them like a crown, a bouquet, proof of love.

When I left my hand on her arm a bit longer than normal, she flipped that arm over my shoulder, standing there holding me like best friends do. My father discussed the finer points of the competition, the teenage boy who had been Zoe's biggest competitor, how it looked when he wiped out during a crossover in the last race.

"It was a piece of cake," she kept saying. And then, "Speaking of cake," over and over.

My family laughed every time.

My mother saved her a big slice, heavy with icing. Zoe ate it standing in the picnic shelter, lake water puddling at her feet, chocolate all over her face and hands. "I can wash off in the lake," she said, when I brought her napkins. She was happy, I could tell, and proud of her success, that all the training paid off.

But when she looked at me, there was worry in the back of her eyes. And even though I was proud too, I was still so angry, so sad, I could hardly meet her gaze.

"Happy birthday to you," Sammy sang, and Zoe grinned at me, her teeth covered with cake and pretty gross. She tried to sing the last part, "Happy birthday, dear Molly," emphasizing the "dear," but her mouth was too full and her eyes too strained.

"We're going to Nicola's on the way home," Anna said. She looked around, located Sarah who was standing as close to Chad as he'd allow. "Molly's birthday dinner."

"It's a tradition," my mother said, her arm around me suddenly in a squeeze. I tried to smile back at her. "You're welcome to come, Zoe."

"Sarah could ride with Chad and Phil," Anna said, pushing her frizzy hair away from her face. "We could take Zoe."

I thought of three hours wedged against Zoe's body, falling asleep on her shoulder. How it might be the last time.

"I just have to negotiate with Chad," Zoe said.

My mother let me go and picked up Sammy. He held his stuffed bear, burrowed deeper into her arms, still singing "Happy birthday" to himself, almost asleep. My mother hefted his little body, settling it comfortably. He'd eaten two huge slices of cake and two hot dogs cooked on the grill. I could tell from his slightly dirty face that he was really back with us, recovering just like everybody. It was only me who didn't fit now.

"I need to change," Zoe said. "And pack my stuff up."

My father was looking up at the sky, thick with gray clouds. "Better hustle," he said. "It's going to let loose and I'd like to be on the highway and off these dirt roads when it does."

We made it back to Lake Placid in record time, the rain following us the entire way. For my birthday dinner I ordered the calamari, a disgusting food when a person thought about it, but at Nicola's they fried it very crisp and served it with a spicy marinara sauce and it was great. Opening presents, I was feeling slightly better. A cool set of Unison pastels from my dad and mom. A CD from Sarah. An envelope from Anna that said "Open later," but I sneaked a peek—it was a round-trip bus ticket to New York City. "We'll go see the sights," she said, her eyes sad and sparkling all at once. "Thanks," I said, trying not to cry in front of everyone. My mother smiled at me, and I knew that when I told her about Zoe and me, she'd be totally Okay. Maybe my dad would even accept us, after everything that had happened.

Before dessert, Zoe gave me her present: a little gold charm and bracelet. The charm had a pair of tiny water skis on a thin loop.

"Will you wear it?" she asked.

I held out my wrist reluctantly, and she slipped the chain around it, clasping the end. The water skis dangled and tickled my arm.

"Very pretty," my mother said. Anna nodded.

"Thanks," I said.

Zoe leaned over and hugged me. When her lips were closest to my ear, she said, "Wear it always."

"I can't believe you haven't seen your mother in years, dear." My mother was wiping Sammy's chin. "That must've been awful. When she left." Her eyes flickered to Anna's, mine. Then she smiled at me reassuringly.

"I didn't blame her." Zoe's voice was matter-of-fact. "My dad was better then."

"He's quite the character now," my aunt said.

"His family's from around here?" My father motioned to the

waiter. "We're going to need more water," he said.

The conversation went on around me, but I didn't pay attention. Over the candle flame, I studied the angle of Zoe's cheekbones, how her gray ocean eyes reflected every bit of light, how she chattered with my family, easy as she usually was with people. When the plates were cleared, she whispered something to my mother and asked the waiter for two crème caramels and to put a candle in one.

I'd eaten too much cake at Daggett Lake, but Zoe fed me spoonfuls of the custardy cream and I tried to swallow, almost gagging on the sweet taste. After a few bites, I shook my head. "It's too much," I said.

"Never too much," Zoe said. She finished off my crème caramel and hers too, then she put down her spoon.

My parents were turned away, holding hands, my mother listening to my dad describe an art show he had been accepted into the following summer. Anna had pulled out a coloring book and Sammy was grabbing crayons from a plastic box. I fingered the water ski charm, let the gold of it flash in the candlelight.

"It's going to be Okay, Molly." Zoe leaned toward me, searching my face. "I promise."

I let the bracelet slide up and down my arm.

She reached over and settled the tiny waterskis at the narrowest part of my wrist. "Sweet sixteen is supposed to be a really great year. It sure was for me."

I looked down at my plate. I could feel a sheen of moisture on my forehead, like I'd just come up from underwater, so I wiped my face with the big white restaurant napkin. "I guess I really did eat too much cake. Or else I'm coming down with something."

I didn't say I was coming down with a broken heart, but Zoe shifted in her chair. When she looked at me again, the gray of her eyes, a gray that redheads almost never have, was flecked with deep unfathomable blue like a ring of mountain shadows.

Chapter 45

I saw Zoe off on the Trailways bus the week we closed up the Cloud Lake cabin. Phil flew out of Montreal the day before, rushing to get to his movie. Since the competition, Zoe had been on the phone almost every night with her mother.

My mother thought it was wonderful. "They haven't seen each other in how many years?" Her eyes were misty.

"I don't know. A long time." Zoe had been ten when her mother ran away with her lover, but I didn't tell my mom that. "She had a nanny, but basically she grew up on her own. Her mother fell in love with someone and had to leave."

I watched her as I said this.

"That can happen," my mother said. But her face looked so peaceful, I knew she wasn't talking about herself.

Chad had driven the SUV home from Daggett Lake, Phil passed out in the backseat. They'd had to pull over to let Phil throw up in the brush on the side of Interstate 87. We were all glad Zoe rode home with us. My mother was glad she wasn't going back to Hollywood with Phil Novato.

"It's not Hollywood, Mom, it's Pasadena." But my mother didn't care. It was all California to her.

At the bus station, Zoe and I stood in the bathroom stall, holding each other for at least an hour. Chad, neat as always in pressed jeans and bright blue T-shirt, had driven us into Plattsburgh and said to take our time, he'd wait outside.

I kept trying to get Zoe to change her mind, but she just kissed me senseless. "Write me," she said, lips moving against my cheek. "Some of those poems of yours. Send me pictures of you dancing."

It was hard trying to stay mad when my face was so wet. "I don't dance. You know that."

"Well, start," she said, "for me."

I moved away, and our skin made a little sucking sound. "I can't promise." Then, suddenly panicked, "I gave you my phone number at the house, didn't I? We'll be in Jay after Tuesday."

"I've got it right here." She patted her jeans pocket. "I don't want you to forget me. All those beautiful girls in your school, a new class. You'll be a junior. Wow."

I couldn't let myself think of New York City, a city full of girls who had no problem kissing someone with red hair and gray eyes. "You're going to graduate in a year. What about that?"

"I won't ever forget you, Molly Fisher," she said.

"I won't let you." I was suddenly less mad, more determined. People had long-distance love affairs all the time. It could work.

"Can you promise that?"

"I promise." I yanked another wad of Kleenex from my jeans pocket, scrubbed my face, then mopped her cheeks. Zoe had wet eyes too but she cried silent and neat, not like me. I reached into my pocket and pulled out the rose quartz fish, handed it to her.

"You're returning it?" she said.

"Just till I see you again. It'll be like a talisman." I stuck my hands in my now-empty pockets. "When do you get in?"

"Three," she said. Her voice got light, happy. "My mother says my room is all ready."

I thought of our room, our bed. I wanted to scream, bury my head in her sweatshirt. *Nonono, you have to stay here, what am I going to do without you, now that everything's different, what am I going to do?* But I just said, "A real reunion."

"You guys close up the cabin tomorrow?" she said.

"We're going camping at Listener Pond. Our last campout of the season." I made a face. "Tradition."

"You don't like it?" Zoe was checking her watch. "I think it would be a blast."

"We all share a tent," I said. "Sammy kicks."

With static so loud we both jumped, an announcement blared through the tiny space. "New York City express. Boarding ten minutes. Platform five."

"That's me," Zoe said. She pulled me against her again, hugging me so tight I couldn't breathe. "Wipe those beautiful eyes. Chad will know for sure."

I opened the stall door and walked to the sinks, splashed cold water on my face. My mascara had run. I patted under my eyes with more Kleenex until the black rings were gone. I didn't wear mascara much, but I wanted her to remember me beautiful.

So much for that, I thought.

Zoe came up behind me and rested her chin on my shoulder, looking at both our faces. Her red hair mingled with my brown. Our eyes were even more alike now. Her skin was tanner than mine, her face leaner. One year older. So many years older inside.

"I love you," she said softly. "Molly Fisher."

Chapter 46

We camped as close to the water as we could, the night after we closed up, after the dock came in and the float where Sammy's Merganser ducks sat, after my father had packed his summer studio and emptied the main room of the cabin of winter paintings. He drove trip after trip back to Jay, bringing our summer lives into our regular lives.

On the last trip, we piled in with our camping equipment and headed toward Listener.

It wasn't much of a place, after Cloud Lake. I didn't know why we went there each year, except my mother and father had stayed there their first overnight together. It was a wildlife preserve, high in the Adirondack Park, and birds of all kinds flocked in to sit in the shallow lake and make their nests. Listener didn't get loons, but it got a lot of other species. Plus all sorts of animals. Sammy was hoping to see a bobcat, but my father said they weren't around much at all anymore.

We partitioned the big camping tent as best we could, my mother and father along one side, with a sheet hung between them and us. Sammy and I had camping cots and sleeping bags. We roasted hot dogs and marshmallows, made s'mores and sang songs. I was too sad to sing much. Sammy sang loud and remembered most of the words to our favorites, which made my mother smile all evening.

It was hard to fall asleep. Sammy snored and shifted on the cot next to me. My parents murmured in the dark. The pond lapped a few feet away, stirred by night wind. Finally the wind quieted, and I heard my mother's breathing. Deep in the woods, a bird called.

I was restless. My head ached and I missed Zoe.

"It's not far to find me," Zoe had said. She had grinned at me, leaning against the bathroom wall. "It's not like I'm running off. We'll see each other soon."

Soon was next month, a whole three weeks away. Anna promised to take me into the city, and I knew I would tell her about Zoe and that it would be Okay. In the meantime school was starting. We'd begin our winter lives again in the big farmhouse. The accident would fade into our history. And I'd begin getting used to living each day without breathing the particular scent of Zoe's skin.

Thinking about Zoe, so many miles from this place, made me itch all over. The only comfortable position I could find was on my back.

"Settle down there, Molly," my father whispered from across the tent. I tried to lie quietly in the flannel-lined bag, thinking of the next morning when maybe we'd swim, or fish or do something that would remind me why I had to stay here.

My mother had started me on ballet lessons when I was just Sammy's age. In the yellow tutu at my first recital, I had actually performed a grand jeté, much to my own and my teacher's astonishment. I remembered how I lay in bed each night for weeks before that recital, practicing, my feet moving into first position, then second, all the way to fifth. If I did it slowly, my feet didn't get tangled in the covers.

So that night at Listener Pond, I imagined Zoe, my almost-promise. Because of this, I practiced again until I finally fell asleep with one foot tucked over the other on its way to third.

In the middle of the night, the moon woke me. From my cot through the screened flap of the tent I could see my father's truck outside, bleached clean, as if God had poured thick white light over everything—the few feet of grassy slope down to the pond, our tent and sleeping bags, the remains of our campfire.

The night air was fragrant with mountain cedar and approaching winter. I could hear the pond moving against its shoreline with the same little laps Cloud Lake made, sounds not unlike a cat drinking from a water bowl.

But I was tired. And although the moonlight was bright, I closed my eyes against it and began to drift off again.

Suddenly I woke. There was a strange noise right outside the tent, near the pond's edge. It sounded like footfalls: a soft thump-thump, a pause, then thump-thump again.

I lifted my head. My parents were sleeping. Sammy was finally quiet. Over the noises outside I could hear his breathing, even and slow. I carefully pulled down the zipper of the sleeping bag and slipped both legs over the edge of the cot until my toes met the ground cloth. Then I raised up and stood in the moonlight.

Thump-thump. I could still hear it, coming from the curve of open space by the shore.

The screen flap rustled only once as I eased it open and stepped onto the dirt path. Pine needles bit into my bare feet. The moon carved a swatch of white to the water, and I ducked behind a tree, not wanting whatever was making the thumping noise to spot me from the clearing, which was still hidden from my view.

As I slid closer, the thump-thump changed. It was now followed by a hiss, a sound like fast breathing. I hid myself next to a big white pine, the sap gluing to my pajamas, wondering whether to go ahead or run back to the tent and safety.

I heard another noise behind me. Turned.

It was my father.

His head was cocked to one side, listening. He reached down very slowly and took my hand in his, like he had when I was a child. We moved forward in our bare feet, scrunching pine needles but making no noise at all compared to the thumps ahead.

When he saw what was in the clearing, delight passed across my father's face. His eyes looked wholly alive, his mouth made a soft O of wonder. He put his finger to his lips.

Five jackrabbits were circled up, taking turns leaping into the air as high as they could, then falling lightly on their back feet— thump—and on their front paws—thump. Their fur glittered in the white light that bathed the open ground like it had bathed our beds, and my father and I were statues in the beautiful dream of their dance.

Then something caught me up too. Maybe it was my promise to myself, dancing again like Zoe did that first time I saw her, freedom in every part of her body. Maybe it was just a memory embedded in my bones. But I felt that freedom suddenly, and ever so slowly, I let go of my father's hand.

I raised my arms up into the gentle arc of first position. My feet followed. Then a shift, to second. Third. At fourth I began to feel the moon seep under my skin, like the jackrabbits must have felt too. It made me forget everything, all the sadness, and it made me fearless. I swept from fifth into a grand jeté.

For a moment I was in the air along with one of them, both of us bathed in moonlight and surrounded by the fertile scent of water and pines. As I landed ever so lightly on the pine needles— thump-thump in my bare feet—the rabbit did as well.

All five jackrabbits turned and stared at us. I looked back at my father who was motionless behind me, the breeze lifting his hair into kind disarray. His eyes were intent, astonished.

A stronger gust came up from the water and goose bumps blew across my skin. The rabbits scattered toward the pond, leaping and racing each other. We watched the last of them, moon-bleached flashes of tail and angled limb, disappear into the scrubby pines that lined the shore.

Above us, the sky was pale and waiting, a temporary mirror for the coming dawn. My father reached for my hand and held it. We stood there, watching the pond slowly brighten, listening to the first morning birds begin. My father's hand was warm and he held mine tightly in his soft and talented fingers. After a few moments, I let go, turning back toward the tent where my mother and brother slept unaware. I walked alone, unexpected lightness still inside my chest, as if the rabbits had released all my longing into the air. Even my feet moved differently.

"Wait up, Molly," my father called softly and my steps slowed automatically.

When I turned back, he was coming toward me, light shining from his face. Above the pond, a few salmon sunrise clouds were forming.

It looked like it was going to be a beautiful day.

The End

Publications from Spinsters Ink
P.O. Box 242
Midway, Florida 32343
Phone: 800-301-6860
www.spinstersink.com

ACROSS TIME by Linda Kay Silva. If you believe in soul
mates, if you know you've had a past life, then join Jessie in the
first of a series of adventures that takes her *Across Time*.
ISBN 978-1883523-91-6 $14.95

SELECTIVE MEMORY by Jennifer L. Jordan. A Kristin
Ashe Mystery. A classical pianist, who is experiencing profound
memory loss after a near-fatal accident, hires private investigator
Kristin Ashe to reconstruct her life in the months leading up to
the crash. ISBN 978-1-883523-88-6 $14.95

HARD TIMES by Blayne Cooper. Together, Kellie and Lorna
navigate through an oppressive, hidden world where lines
between right and wrong blur, sexual passion is forbidden but
explosive, and love is the biggest risk of all.
ISBN 978-1-883523-90-9 $14.95

THE KIND OF GIRL I AM by Julia Watts. Spanning decades,
The Kind of Girl I Am humorously depicts an extraordinary
woman's experiences of triumph, heartbreak, friendship and
forbidden love. ISBN 978-1-883523-89-3 $14.95

PIPER'S SOMEDAY by Ruth Perkinson. It seemed as though
life couldn't get any worse for feisty, young Piper Leigh Cliff
and her three-legged dog, Someday. ISBN 978-1-883523-87-9
$14.95

MERMAID by Michelene Esposito. When May unearths a box
in her missing sister's closet she is taken on a journey through
her mother's past that leads her not only to Kate but to the
choices and compromises, emptiness and fullness, the beauty
and jagged pain of love that all women must face.
ISBN 978-1-883523-85-5 $14.95

NIGHT DIVING by Michelene Esposito. Night Diving is both a young woman's coming-out story and a thirty-something coming-of-age journey that proves you can go home again. ISBN 978-1-883523-52-7 $14.95

ASSISTED LIVING by Sheila Ortiz-Taylor. Violet March, an eighty-two-year-old resident of Casa de los Sueños, finally has the opportunity to put years of mystery reading to practical use. One by one her comrades, the Bingos, are dying. Is this natural attrition, or is there a sinister plot afoot? ISBN 978-1-883523-84-2 $14.95

FURTHEST FROM THE GATE by Ann Roberts. *Furthest from the Gate* is a humorous chronicle of a woman's coming of age, her complicated relationship with her mother and the responsibilities to family that last a lifetime. ISBN 978-1-883523-81-7 $14.95

EYES OF GRAY by Dani O'Connor. Grayson Thomas was the typical college senior with typical friends, a typical job and typical insecurities about her future. One Sunday morning, Gray's life became a little less typical, she saw a man clad in black, and started doubting her own sanity. ISBN 978-1-883523-82-4 $14.95

ORDINARY FURIES by Linda Morgenstein. Tired of hiding, exhausted by her grief after her husband's death, Alexis Pope plunges into the refreshingly frantic world of restaurant resort cooking and dining in the funky chic town of Guerneville, California. ISBN 978-1-883523-83-1 $14.95

A POEM FOR WHAT'S HER NAME by Dani O'Connor. Professor Dani O'Connor had pretty much resigned herself to the fact that there was no such thing as a complete woman. Then out of nowhere, along comes a woman who blows Dani's theory right out of the water. ISBN 1-883523-78-8 $14.95

DISORDERLY ATTACHMENTS by Jennifer L. Jordan. The fifth Kristin Ashe Mystery. Kris investigates whether a mansion someone wants to convert into condos is haunted. ISBN 1-883523-74-5 $14.95

WOMEN'S STUDIES by Julia Watts. With humor and heart, *Women's Studies* follows one school year in the lives of three young women and shows that in college, one's extracurricular activities are often much more educational than what goes on in the classroom. ISBN 1-883523-75-3 $14.95

VERA'S STILL POINT by Ruth Perkinson. Vera is reminded of exactly what it is that she has been missing in life. ISBN 1-883523-73-7 $14.95

OUTRAGEOUS by Sheila Ortiz-Taylor. Arden Benbow, a motorcycle riding, lesbian Latina poet from LA is hired to teach poetry in a small liberal arts college in northwest Florida. ISBN 1-883523-72-9 $14.95

UNBREAKABLE by Blayne Cooper. The bonds of love and friendship can be as strong as steel. But are they unbreakable? ISBN 1-883523-76-1 $14.95

ALL BETS OFF by Jaime Clevenger. Bette Lawrence is about to find out how hard life can be for someone of low society standing in the 1900s. ISBN 1-883523-71-0 $14.95

UNBEARABLE LOSSES by Jennifer L. Jordan. The fourth Kristin Ashe Mystery. Two elderly sisters have hired Kris to discover who is pilfering from their award-winning holiday display. ISBN 1-883523-68-0 $14.95

EXISTING SOLUTIONS by Jennifer L. Jordan. The second Kristin Ashe Mystery. When Kris is hired to find an activist's biological father, things get complicated when she finds herself falling for her client. ISBN 1-883523-69-9 $14.95

A SAFE PLACE TO SLEEP by Jennifer L. Jordan. The first Kristin Ashe Mystery. Kris is approached by well-known lesbian Destiny Greaves with an unusual request. One that will lead Kris to hunt for her own missing childhood pieces. ISBN 1-883523-70-2 $14.95